A FORGOTTEN PAST
STALKS THE FUTURE

A row of dark heads appeared over the roadside embankment. Heads and shoulders, eyes, low brows. Scrutinizing the group of tourists. Regarding the wrecked bus. Nobody moved. Metal crackled.

The tourists shrank away, closing ranks. They were confronting something which filled them with an overwhelming sense of dread. Never before in their lives had they confronted the unknown. This demon—its darting gaze, its stance—challenged the rules they lived by.

The animal was 1.5 meters high. It remained where it was, in a crouch, content, master of the situation. Two of its fellows scrambled up the bank and joined it standing slightly to its rear. The three of them waited, teeth bared, snouts twitching. Now, a dozen of them climbed nimbly up, to stand behind their leader. Their confidence was growing. They dared to look away from the tourists, grunting to each other and licking their furry, murderous lips.

BRIAN ALDISS

ENEMIES OF THE SYSTEM

A TALE OF HOMO UNIFORMIS

 AVON
PUBLISHERS OF BARD, CAMELOT AND DISCUS BOOKS

Portions of this work originally appeared in *Cosmos.*

AVON BOOKS
A division of
The Hearst Corporation
959 Eighth Avenue
New York, New York 10019

First Avon Printing, February, 1981

AVON TRADEMARK REG. U.S. PAT. OFF. AND IN
OTHER COUNTRIES, MARCA REGISTRADA,
HECHO EN U.S.A.

Printed in the U.S.A.

*For my esteemed friend Jon Bing
in his Northern fastness*

Have you heard
That silence where the birds are dead yet something
pipeth like a bird?

I

Inspirational music played as they moved from the terminal buildings into the ferry.

Without fuss, without pushing, they settled into relaxers and waited for the ferry to depart. Fifty-two of them took their places, the sexes about equally balanced. Their clothes were so similar in cut, and so subdued in color and material, as to resemble a uniform; their hair, whether male or female, was trimmed to approximately the same length; their faces were all bland, even blank. They sat without restlessness. They were the élite of the system, allowed to vacation on the Classified planet of Lysenka II.

The ferry rose silently, dead on time. World Peace City, the Earth itself, shrank behind them. They watched the planet dwindle, then turned and smiled circumspectly at each other. They were strangers and nobody knew who was who; even among the élite there were many power grades.

From the ferry, the passengers transferred to a gulf-hopper awaiting them in a parking orbit round the Moon. As soon as the ferry dropped away, the gulfhopper established a charm-field and began its expensive cratobatics. Earth disappeared like an eyeball dropping down a drain; the sun was transformed into an icicle of light, and vanished. Time became a series of equations.

Oblivious to alarm, the tourists could now settle down and become acquainted with one another. The distance from the Solar System to the Lysenka System was 50.2 light years, in Ordinary Space terms, so passengers had forty hours on the transference from system to system in which to indulge in social intercourse or related activities.

The gulfhopper was a spacious craft, well provided with lounges, restaurants, view-chambers, an aquatics suite, and private rooms. Most of the tourists, being important people, kept their importance in repair by walking about the public rooms in a dignified manner. Hostesses in blue Gulfways uniform assisted some passengers to meet the partners that Extra-System selectors had chosen for them, if they had not had time to meet before embarking at World Peace City.

One of the smiling hostesses introduced two tall people, a man and a woman, who briefly touched fingertips and then stood regarding each other. Nodding, the hostess left them to themselves.

"My name is Jerezy Kordan, World Citizen 692," the male said, smiling to soften the familiarity of using only his last three numbers on first meeting. "I am pleased that we are to be associated for this vacation."

The female smiled back and was just as informal. "I'm World Citizen 194, Millia Sygiek. And I'm pleased that the selector picked you, Utopianist Kordan, since I know that we are going to be compatible."

Kordan had a long serious face with thick lips which were generally pursed, and long grey eyes. He stood squarely before her, his hands hanging relaxedly by his side.

Sygiek was almost as tall as he, a woman with light brown hair and grey eyes. Her jaw was firm, her expression a little severe until she smiled. She folded her hands and held them at waist level as they talked.

"We could be nothing but compatible since the computer graded us for compatibility. Compatibility is a quality we both rate as desirable," she said.

"Inevitably. Pleasure is stipulated as one of the factors of our vacation, and so compatibility is part of the guarantee. Don't you find compatibility a positive quality, a constructive quality?"

"I was meaning only to imply that some Progressives regard the male–female relationship as a little old-fashioned,

10

even irrelevant to the needs of the system: they question the useful function of gender."

He gestured slightly with his hands. "We tolerate Progressives in our world society." He spoke without any particular emphasis. "But of course they form only approximately 1.45 per cent of the population." He took her arm as if dismissing that subject.

They were on their way toward their private room when a tenor voice said softly over the artificial pulse-beats, "Remember that sexual intercourse is an approved social usage. It is pleasurable. Inevitably, it increases the physical and mental well-being of both partners, thus enhancing their value to the system. Associate with your partner as much as possible on the journey. Happy lying!"

Sygiek smiled. "You see, like good utopianists, our wishes run ahead of the official reminder."

But, as they passed through one of the relaxation halls, they were distracted for a moment. A row of chessputers sat before a row of three-dimensional chess boards, waiting to play against any human who cared to challenge them. Each chessputer was smaller than a person's head; its single arm, of a flesh-like substance, folded down into its side when it was out of action. Someone had pushed two of the machines together and they were playing the complex game against each other.

As one game was won, the machines solemnly reset the pieces and moved straight into the next. Several tourists were watching.

Peering over the shoulder of one of the onlookers, Kordan said, "That's amusing! You see they exert their capacities merely to win against each other."

The man in front of him—a stocky dark-featured man of less than average height—looked round and said, "It would be more amusing if one of them showed a little glee at winning."

When they were settled in their comfortable room, Kordan said, "What could that man have meant, that it would have been more amusing if the machines showed a little pleasure at winning? How can a machine be expected to show pleasure?"

" 'Glee.' He said, 'glee.' "

She began to undress.

He was following his own train of thought. "One does inevitably experience some pleasure in winning, yet 'Our strength lies in our unity.' A valuable adage. Winning implies competition, whilst unity implies no competition. It is a slight paradox. Since we are privileged to vacation on Lysenka II, we are among the winners of the system. May I express it like that?"

"There is always privilege involved in visiting an extrasolar planet. In the case of Lysenka II, I gather that it has been opened to tourism before complete conformity with cultural standards has been attained—simply in order to join in the anniversary celebrations."

"It is true that the animal life has not been subdued, as it will inevitably have to be." His lips twitched. "For me as an historian, with special interest in the pre-utopian world, I welcome a chance to see something of a planet where the animal societies, as I understand, approximate to what life used to be on Earth before Biocom."

Sygiek removed her stockings as he began to slip out of his one-piece tunic. "My business is entirely with the present. I have no interest in the pre-utopian world, not even in this anniversary year." She spoke briskly.

He smiled by pursing his lips. "Perhaps Lysenka II will awaken new interests. Undoubtedly, we shall see sights incompatible with civilization. So until then, let us refresh ourselves with some compatibility. Kindly move over and open your legs."

She smiled and relaxed against the voluptuous cushions, readying herself for him like a mare for her rider. Unbidden, a picture of the man by the chessputers came to her mind.

"Let's have a little *glee*," she said.

All too soon, the beautiful expensive structure had crossed that gulf of light which even the world state would never subjugate. It materialized in orbit about Lysenka II, while almost sub-vocal commentaries uttered facts about the sun, Lysenka, and its four attendant planets: three of them swirling globes of gas, and only II a world remotely suitable for the establishment of law and enlightenment.

In the ferry on the way down to Peace City, the one base so far constructed on Lysenka II, the commentaries welcomed their guests.

"We hope that you will be happy during your stay on Lysenka II, and your intellects fully engaged. Although this planet has been known to the world state for many centuries, it is only just being opened up for tourism. You may regard yourself as especially privileged to be here. For those of us who work in Lysenka II, it is an honor to greet you, knowing as we do that you are part of the special System-wide celebrations of the one millionth anniversary of the establishment of Biocom. The universal beneficial aspects of Biocom will never be more appreciated than on this planet, where everything is primitive, regressive, and of an entirely lower politico-evolutionary order.

"So we trust that you will enjoy your stay and be strengthened by it for further dedication to our beloved system. Welcome to Lysenka II."

The passengers looked at each other. Some smiled guardedly.

Everyone was given booster and acupunctural shots to acclimatize them to the planet before they settled on alien soil. Down swooped the ferry. A moment of silence more dreadful than any gulf of light, and then great exit doors swung open. They opened too rapidly: the sky was a bright tan ceiling of cloud, enclosing the visitors on the new world. They blinked, unaccountably reluctant to move forward.

Hostesses, in red Outourist uniform instead of Gulfways blue, ushered the tourists into LDBs, smiling and reassuring them. As soon as a long-distance bus was full, it began to accelerate down one of the radial roads leading from Peace City into the wilderness.

The passengers took deep breaths and looked at each other, as if the new environment forced them to take fresh measure of themselves. In the unaccustomed light, the set of their faces was strange.

The bus arrived at Dunderzee in under an E-hour. Dunderzee was Lysenka's newly opened tourist resort. It stood on the edge of territory no human had explored from the ground.

Still reassuringly chaperoned, the tourists were conducted to their rooms in the Unity Hotel. The hotel was sumptuous but not entirely finished. Every room, besides a spectacular view of the broken, tawny country outside, boasted a living wall which showed a close-up of Dunderzee Lake. As Kordan and Sygiek entered their room, they felt compelled to stand before the wall and gaze at the waterfall that fed the lake. With slow thunder, the water dropped free from almost one thousand meters down the carmine sides of Dunderzee Gorge. Cumbersome birds glided down the face of the gorge, dipping into the column of white water, flashing in the spray.

Turning away to place his kit on the shelf, Kordan said, "Though I have traveled most of the System, and twice visited the Argyre Ocean since they released the waters, Dunderzee Gorge impresses me. We shall enjoy visiting the reality."

She was surprised that he spoke so subjectively, and said nothing, standing to watch a pack of man-like creatures which swam strongly in the foam of the lake.

"Millia, tell me more about yourself," Kordan said.

"You can judge me for yourself." She met his eyes. Both were silent, contemplating each other.

"Where were you born? On Earth?" he inquired.

"I was born in a township on the Ust'-Urt Plateau, two hundred and fifty kilometers from the Aral Sea." She indicated the falling water, the troubled lake. "I never saw anything but flatness until I was twelve years old, so perhaps this great gorge strikes me as against nature. It's unsophisticated, I can see that."

"The day after tomorrow, you and I shall stand beside that waterfall in reality, Millia."

"Yes, that should be a worthwhile cultural expedition. Also I wish to become more acquainted with our fellow tourists. They form an interesting cross-section of the middle echelons of our system society. You may escort me down to the bar, if you wish."

"Let's stay alone here together, Millia. I enjoy your company. There will be time for the others tomorrow, inevitably."

14

"Don't utter anti-social remarks. Unity is a quality which needs perpetual renewal. We had a good time alone on the gulfhopper. Now let's integrate with our new community."

He looked back longingly at the waterfall as they left the room.

II

The Unity Hotel held some two thousand guests, all of them important in their own right, back in the System. Jerezy Kordan was an historian specializing in the Classified period of pre-utopian Europe before the introduction of Biocom. He was a full Academician of the IPUS, the Institute of Pre-Utopian Studies, and likely to rise to Chancellor in time. Millia Sygiek announced herself as a commutation supervisor with System Population Mobility. As such, it was her job to travel the planets and satellites of the System, seeing that communities remained balanced in size and genetic heritage and did not degenerate; the enormous task of controlling migratory circulation fell to her and the SPM bureau.

During the afternoon, freshly arrived tourists were encouraged to walk in the safety of the grounds of the hotel, to accustom themselves to gravity, atmosphere, and angstrom differences. There was much to see, including a zoo which housed some of the autochthonous species of Lysenka. Sygiek and Kordan teamed up with another couple of tourists, an exobotanist called Ian Takeido, a quiet young man who had spent most of his life in the Jovian sub-system, and Jaini Regentop, a pallid girl who was a DNA specialist on the Technoeugenics Advisory Council.

The voice of a commentator, deep and paternal, followed them as they walked down one of the broad avenues of the zoo.

"Most of the trees on either side of you are classified as Lysenkan calamites, or horsetails. Their structure is very similar to that of trees which grew on Earth during the Carboniferous Age. Always remember that Lysenka II is only just emerging from its equivalent of the Devonian Age and entering its own Carboniferous. In other words, it is at the same stage of development as was Earth some 370 million years ago.

"You will already have noticed the trees we call cage trees. Such phyla never developed on Earth. Each tree is in fact a small colony of trees of up to fifteen in number. Their trunks grow first outward from a common base, then upward. Then, as they age, the trunks curl inward again, to meet in a knot of foliage some twelve feet above the ground. So a cage is formed—hence their name." The voice deepened into a chuckle. "We like to think that this habit of unity makes the cage trees the first example of socialist unity to be found in the vegetable world on Lysenka."

"Charming," Jaini Regentop said. "Charming. Such a constructive little joke, too."

That evening, the council of the Unity Hotel held a grand reception, with a banquet and many toasts and speeches, followed by dancing and a folk group brought over from Bohemia City on Titan.

Next morning, when the tourists stirred, it was to find that their living walls were blank, and their radio and vision screens not functioning. Only the internal communications of the hotel still operated. An embarrassed management council put out a hasty apology and explained why.

"The temporary suspension of external communications will in no way affect the expedition to Dunderzee Gorge planned for today. The LDBs, your vehicles, are micro-nuclear-powered. Unfortunately, all our communications are via comsat, while most of the power is beamed from the sun Lysenka to us also by satellite; these functions are in suspension temporarily, owing to a strike at Satellite Control in Peace City. We are happy to say that the hotel has its own power store with plentiful reserves for a week. Meanwhile, we apologize for any inconvenience and the loss of your living walls. As guests will appreciate, Lysenka

18

II is a very primitive planet, which sometimes has its effect on the natures of people. Thank you."

The guests regarded one another unappreciatively.

"The powermen and the satellite engineers are trying to renegotiate their contract with the Planetary Praesidium," Ian Takeido told Kordan and Sygiek in a low voice, over breakfast. "I was talking to one of the hotel's technicians last night. It seems that because they are working on an extra-solar planet, they have to serve a full ten-year term before returning to the System. They want the term reduced to seven years."

"Gulfhopping is considerably expensive, you know," Sygiek said mildly.

"But *striking!*" Regentop exclaimed, looking over her coffee cup. "How primitive—Ian had to explain the term to me. I thought the penalty for striking was . . ." She let her voice tail away.

"If you want something, then you have to negotiate for it," said Kordan. "A platitude, but true."

"They got tired of negotiating," said Takeido. "I hope you don't mind my speaking so freely, but they've been negotiating for years, to no effect."

"But public life is negotiation, as long as it does not interfere with the march of government," said Kordan. "The process is part of a general dialectic."

Takeido shook his head.

"These technicians see it as an emotional matter. What they are saying is, 'Earth is our Id—we must have it or die.' "

" 'Id!' Another word I had never heard before," complained Regentop, laughing and looking anxiously at their faces.

"As an academician, I can assure you that it is an archaic word indeed," said Kordan, pursing his lips. "And in this case almost inevitably misused."

"Probably declared a non-word," said Sygiek, regarding the others in turn. "In which case, it should be neither used nor misused." She frowned.

There was a pause. Regentop leaned forward confidentially.

"Use your authority to explain to us what 'id' means, Jerezy Kordan," she said. "We are all of the élite—and out

of the System. No harm can be done by a little talk here."
She looked excited and smiled nervously at him as she
spoke.

Sygiek folded her hands in her lap and looked out of the
tall windows. "If words drop out of use, there is generally
good reason for it," she said warningly. "They may serve as
counters in subversive systems of thought. You understand
that well, Jerezy Kordan."

"In this case, the explanation is only instructive," Kordan said placatingly. She continued to stare out of the
windows. He turned to the others. "Id was an entity of
ancient superstition, like a ghost. Briefly, long ago in the
epoch before the advent of Biocom, several perverted inter-
pretations of the nature of man flourished. Most of them
assumed that man was not a rational economic being. Such
may arguably have been the case before communalism
provided him with the necessary rational sociopolitical
framework within which he could function as a unit. 'Id'
was a term coined by one of those perverted interpreta-
tions—a particularly pernicious system, a blind alley of
thought which, I'm happy to say, was always opposed,
even by our first communist ancestors."

He had fallen into an easy lecture style. Sygiek looked
down; the others stared at his face with some admiration.
Kordan continued, "In those bygone days, the physiological conflict between the brain, the central nervous
system, and the autonomic nervous system was not understood. Misunderstanding of man's nature inevitably arose.
The physiological conflict was interpreted as psychological,
as originating in some hypothetical depth of the mind.
The mind was regarded as very complex, like a savage
independent world almost. In this erroneous model of human physiology—that's what 'mind' really was—there was
presumed to lurk in its muddy recesses various savage and
socially destructive elements, waiting to overthrow reason.
Those elements were bundled together under the term 'id.'
It was a regressive force."

They had finished their meal. As Takeido pushed the
sofa back, he said, "Instructive! How did the ancient term
materialize here on Lysenka II a million or more years
later, do you suppose, Jerezy Kordan?"

"As I thought I had made clear, the term was coined in

some long-vanished capitalist system—in part to explain and explain away its own organizational deficiencies. If you understand the retrogressive nature of the animals on this world, then you can understand that the—er, striking technicians must have picked up the term here."

"They should be criticized," said Regentop, in a shocked voice. "It all sounds disgracefully non-utopian."

Sygiek stood up and remained looking down on the others, but Takeido leaned forward, clearly wishing to carry the subject further. Clasping his hands together earnestly, he said, "This is most interesting, Jerezy. If you are right—and of course I don't doubt that—then the striking technicians have it wrong. 'Earth is our Id' . . . Lysenka is the subversive forbidden place, so *it* should be the id and Earth should be . . . I don't know the term. I'm just a simple exobotanist."

Regentop patted his back and smiled proudly.

" 'Super-ego,' " said Kordan. "Earth should be the super-ego." He laughed dismissively, disowning the term, and glanced up to see how Sygiek was taking the conversation.

"This discussion is too self-indulgent," she said. " 'Speaking of error is itself error.' Let's finish and get into the buses. Most of the others have already gone ahead."

"These old theories were nonsense, inevitably," Kordan said to her, taking her arm as they left the dining room. "Medieval. Like alchemy."

She regarded him with slightly raised eyebrows and a smile he had not seen before. "But alchemy *led* somewhere, Jerezy Kordan, Academician. It provided one of the foundations of scientific advancement. Whereas psychoanalysis was a dead end."

"Ah ha, then you are also familiar with these ancient and interdicted models. *Psychoanalysis!*"

"It is part of my job to acquaint myself with what is forbidden."

He looked searchingly at her. She met his gaze. He said nothing, and they moved out into the open. Kordan stood on the steps, breathing deeply as he looked ahead.

Buses waited like great slumbering beasts.

The exobotanist, Takeido, caught Kordan's attention, coughed, and said apologetically, "It was a pleasure to listen to you talking at the breakfast table, Jerezy Kordan. Working on the Jovian moons, one is much alone. One thinks, one longs to talk . . . to talk about many things, such as the topics you touched on. May Jaini Regentop and I ride with you to Dunderzee?"

Kordan looked at the youth, as if thinking how young and thin he was. He watched the black eyebrows twitch nervously on Takeido's forehead.

"You are at liberty to choose any seat you wish in the bus," he said. "But language is much more precious and must be guarded. Better to be resolute than curious. 'Resolution is the foe of deviation,' as the saying has it. I imagine that applies as much on Jupiter and Lysenka as on Earth."

"Of course . . ." said Takeido, and swallowed.

"Let's get aboard the buses, then," said Kordan smiling. He nodded at Sygiek. She nodded contentedly back, and they walked down the steps, fully in command of their world, toward the waiting buses.

The gates in the fortified perimeter of the Unity Hotel slid open. Above them fluttered a banner with the device of the United System and the legend:

STRIVE TOWARD THE SECOND MILLION YEARS OF
BIOCOM-UNITY!

As the LBD rolled through the gateway, Sygiek noticed that she was seated next to the stocky man who had made the remarks about chessputers on the gulfhopper not not experiencing glee. He nodded genially, as if they were old companions.

"A session of idle sightseeing!" Sygiek exclaimed to Kordan, turning away from the other man. "I have never done such a thing in my life, and half-doubt the propriety of it now. Days are more to be valued when fruitfully occupied."

Kordan scrutinized her, as if trying to read her thoughts. "Don't reproach yourself with such sentiments, Millia. We are not idle. We are on Lysenka to restore our energies, so that we can return to the System better equipped to work for it and to appreciate its values."

The stocky man leaned forward, clasping his hands between his knees, and said, addressing them both, "Don't be too strict with yourselves, friends. Savor enjoyment as a positive force in its own right. Idleness has virtues of its own."

"Exactly what I meant," said Kordan, pleasantly. "Idleness restores our energies."

The stocky man introduced himself as Vul Dulcifer 057, Chief Engineer responsible for the air-conditioning systems of Iridium, on Venus. He had a big hard head, with big hard features. Gazing out of the window at the passing scenery, he said, "Like everyone else, I am never idle. My work keeps me going thirteen E-hours a day, and I run various committees. 'Utopia is sustained only by hard work'—I know the party slogan, don't remind me. The system's a machine. If a few of us have made it to this Classified planet, with all these degenerate capitalist animals running about, then we are of the élite, and I maintain that we have earned some idleness. I frankly see idleness as a just reward, not simply one more obstacle on the assault course of World Peace."

As she watched and listened to him speaking, Sygiek thought that she and Dulcifer could never be compatible. He was as small and dark as she was tall and pale. He was thickset, with massive shoulders; his every movement expressed energy. The irises of his eyes were a dark sea-blue, rolling between black fringes of eyelash. His dark hair was sparse, and clung close to his square skull. She was aware as she watched the movements of his clearly defined lips of a disturbance within her, a disturbance chased by the reflection, "He regards Kordan and me merely as two standard products of the system, without minds of our own . . ."

"To speak of idleness as a reward can lead swiftly to incorrect thinking, isn't that so, Jerezy? Idleness can be no different on this planet from what it is anywhere in the System: a trap, a bait for deviationist ideas. How can those properties change? Creative idleness is a different matter."

A hostess, rosy of cheek, with long legs and a warm smile, came down in the aisle of the bus, pausing to exchange a word with everyone. She was trim in her red uniform; most of the tourists wore sloppy-maos.

23

"Are you enjoying the primitive landscape?" she asked. "Isn't it charmingly undeveloped? What an inspiring symbol of potential."

"Yes," said Dulcifer. "And at the same time we're exercising our minds like good utopianists with an argument about the nature of idleness."

Takeido and Regentop had been listening from the seat in front. The former turned and said to Dulcifer, "You seem to lack a little data, utopianist. You see, idleness is a physiological malfunction. It's mistaken to treat it as a quality of mind, when injections can cure it as soon as it manifests itself."

As he spoke, he kept glancing at Kordan to see how he was taking this speech.

A bureaucrat by the name of Georg Morits leaned across the aisle and said vehemently, "You're right there, but let me remind you that idleness is still sometimes manifested as a mental quality in unfortunate throw-backs to *homo sapiens*. I know. I have to deal with quite a few committals of that sort of person, in my line of business. I'm in an office in Moscow, you know. The city of cities." They did know. This dull person had been boasting during the banquet of how beautiful it was in Moscow, an old city which had been the capital of the first communist state and many times rebuilt. "You can be legally charged with being a *homo sapien,* you know. It's in the statute banks now."

"Not on Venus, it isn't," said Dulcifer, sturdily. "That's like charging an animal with the offense of being an animal."

They made no response to that. They knew all about Venus, and the devolutionary tendencies of Iridium City.

"We are straying from the point. If I could remind you of the historical background to this argument—" Kordan began; but Sygiek cut him off, saying, "Shall we just forget this silly discussion?"

Kordan looked hurt, but Dulcifer said, smiling to remove the sting from his remark, "You are too repressive for vacation-time, Utopianist Millia Sygiek! I'd like to hear what your companion was going to say. Frankly, scenery bores me—but I've never lost interest in my fellow human beings."

Warmth rose in Sygiek's cheeks. She turned a gaze on him which would have melted iridium but she said nothing.

"I was merely going to say—for the sake of the historical record—that those early genetic engineers who established *homo uniformis,* Man Alike Throughout, were the—"

"Forgive me, Academician Kordan, but I am in techno-eugenics, working on the Central Council," said Jaini Regentop, giving him her polite smile, "and you are not correct in your phraseology. Those genetic engineers were merely instruments of change in the great progression from *homo sapiens* to *homo uniformis;* they took orders. First had to come the immortal work of physiologists and the great endotomists—"

"Jaini, you should not interrupt Jerezy Kordan," said Takeido. "He is an Academician."

"Then he will understand. Between them," said Regentop, adopting something of Kordan's lecturing manner, and addressing her remarks mainly to him, "the endotomists established the fact that man's physiological structure comprised three governance systems which were in conflict. Owing to the rapid evolutionary development of man from animal, those governance systems were not entirely compatible. We might in the same way complain of a machine that it was faulty because it contained too much wiring. The problem was one of efficiency."

Kordan nodded and looked bored, but Regentop pressed on.

"The great endotomists and physiologists developed a method whereby those governance systems could be developed into one harmonious super-system. The three governance systems I refer to, by the way, were known as Central Nervous System, primarily a motor system, Autonomic Nervous System, primarily a sensual system, and Neocortex, primarily a thought system.

"To develop this more reliable super-system, the bioshunt was introduced. As you probably know, the bioshunt—there's been a lot of talk about it in this anniversary year—is an in-built processor which phases out much of the activity of the old autonomic nervous system or renders it subject to the direct control of the thought sys-

25

tem. An obvious example is the penile erection, once an involuntary act.

"I frequently impress on my classes that the bio-shunt is the very basis of our great utopia. It has banished the emotional problems which always plagued *homo sapiens*. Wars, religions, romantic love, mental illness—all manifestations of outmoded physiological systems."

"This is what I mentioned earlier, Millia," Kordan said heavily to Sygiek. "Please continue, Jaini Regentop, if you so wish. You express youself well."

She nodded in humility. "It is my duty to express myself well when speaking of so supreme an achievement. Rationality was something poor *homo sapiens* could never achieve. He was divided against himself physiologically. *Therefore* he was also divided against himself mentally and socially and politically and—well, in every way conceivable. He could not devise a stable society as we have done. Division was his lot."

Her voice took on a quieter note. "Division was his lot. Yet *sapiens* had vision, too. Yes, he even visualized Utopia, the perfect place.

"And, in an ironic way, he achieved Utopia in the end, though it meant his extinction. When his physiotechnicians and early endotomists invented the whole principle of Biological Communism—the theory behind the bio-shunt itself—then it became possible to rationalize the inharmonious governance systems genetically, passing on the improvement to succeeding generations. Through chromosome microsurgery, *sapiens* did away with all manner of systemic weakness—thus eliminating himself and ushering in a virtual new race. A race without absurd evolutionary flaws. A race truly capable of establishing Utopia. In a word, us. *Homo uniformis*, Man Alike Throughout."

They regarded each other's faces, smiling reflectively.

"And what has this ancient tale to do with idleness, except that it is itself an idle tale by now?" asked Dulcifer.

"It's the birth tale of the World State, no less," said Sygiek, frowning.

"Jaini Regentop has just explained," Takeido said to Dulcifer. "Idleness was an old *sapiens* weakness. It sprang from a lack of purpose, no doubt—from internal confusion.

There's no physiological reason for idleness in these enlightened days, utopianist. We've conquered it."

Dulcifer scratched his head. He laughed. "You're a bit young for a conqueror!"

Takeido slipped back into his seat.

"There's a Museum of Homo Sapiens in Moscow," said Georg Morits, adding confidentially, "they were quite advanced for primitives, you know—even had a limited form of space travel—the principles of which were invented in Moscow. I can tell you such things, since you are of the élite, and not of the ignorant. You appreciate them. Ah, it's good to talk among equals."

III

They were sitting talking in the last bus. Three buses moved ahead of them, gradually drawing apart as they gathered speed down the embanked road. The great structure of Unity, which had dominated everything, dwindled behind them, swallowed by the everlasting landscape of Lysenka. Occasionally, as the road rose with the land, they could glimpse the shoulders of a distant plateau, riding above the warm obscurities of the plain.

Kordan clutched Sygiek's hand, but she soon withdrew it.

The hostess in her neat red uniform with the Outourist insignia had exchanged a word with everyone individually. She reached the front of the LDB, where she took up a microphone and addressed the passengers, smiling as she did so.

"Hello, friends of the system, my name is Rubyna Constanza 868, and I have the pleasure of being your guide for today. Welcome to the journey. We shall be away from Unity for two days, and shall spend tonight in comfortable quarters in the Dunderzee Gorge, which I feel sure you will enjoy. We shall view some of the wonders of this planet, and also some of its instructive blemishes. Refreshments will be served when we stop at midday. I am continually at your service. There are service bells by your fingertips."

"She's very pretty," Takeido whispered. Regentop frowned for silence.

"First I would like to remind you of a few facts concerning this planet. You will be familiar with some of them, but facts take life from their substitutes in reality.

"This planet is large by the standards of the System Inner Planets, having an equatorial diameter of approximately 20,000 kilometers. Fortunately its mass is relatively light, so we do not suffer from oppressive gravity. Lysenka II revolves on its axis once every 33.52 E-hours, which makes for an inconveniently long day. You will be able to rest at refreshment-break, since your seats recline fully.

"As we can observe, it is cloudy overhead. The sun rarely shines through in these latitudes, though cloud may clear at evening. Lysenka is rather a warm and drowsy planet at this period of its history."

She indicated the world rolling past their windows. "There is a grove of cage trees to our left. Otherwise, vegetation is sparse. Most of the planet is semi-desert, owing to soil paucity and lack of micro-bacterial activity.

"Although the planet has been discovered for more than a million years, we established a base on it only ten years ago. The planet awaits development. The problem is an ideological one—what to do with the fauna. The World State is still considering this vital matter. Owing to the low energy life systems here, the fauna has not been able to establish itself over much of the globe. It would be possible to extirpate all the animals. That is a neat and attractive solution. On the other hand, they may prove invaluable for studies in behavior, and as a source for laboratory animals, etcetera."

Constanza had slightly hastened this part of her talk. She slowed her delivery again to add, "However, such problems need not enter our heads on your vacation, since the decisions rest with others. At this time, we need only enjoy the strange sights. On your right, you can see now a flock of kangaroo-like creatures. I assure you there is no danger, since we are in constant radio contact with surveillance satellites. Well, that is, just today we are out of touch because of the technical difficulties of the strike; we are out of touch, but in any case we are perfectly safe in the bus. Notice that the creatures are regarding us with respect."

The animals now bounding along beside the road had no tails. Their resemblance to kangaroos began and ended with their small pointed heads and their way of leaping over the ground. For the rest, they were more man-like, and waved their fists with oddly human gestures at the bus as it flashed past.

"These animals eat vegetation and also flesh," said Constanza. "Their turn of speed is mainly to deliver them from those things that desire to eat them."

The bus curved away from the flat and proceeded down a long, well-cambered curve. Ahead loomed a gigantic wall of rock, crowned with fringes of the sappy white-stemmed horsetails. It was growing difficult to understand how the bus could avoid smashing into the rock face when a curve was turned and the vehicle plunged into a tunnel.

The sides of the tunnel were lasered smooth. On the walls, inspiring slogans had been incised, slogans which contributed much to the moral tone of society. For the first time since leaving Unity, all the passengers sat up and paid attention out of the windows, sometimes reading aloud with pleasure words they had known since childhood.

Resolution Is the Foe of Deviation

Unity Breeds Immunity

Never Think What Cannot Be Said

Eternal Vigilance Grants Eternal Security:
Without It Is Eternal Anarchy

There Are No Free Launches

The slogans glowed in enticing colors, smoldering into darkness again as soon as the bus had passed.

Suddenly, they were propelled back into daylight. As the rock fell away and the road ceased to curve, the tourists found themselves traveling over a tremendous plain. Its extent was emphasized by the cliff now falling behind them, and the still-distant plateau in the mists. The floor

31

of the plain—ugly, barren and broken—was dotted with rocky debris which rose in mounds. Now and then, a sluggish river could be glimpsed.

"We have entered the Great Rift Valley," Constanza said. "The Gorge is far ahead of us. In this area, and all the way to the Starinek Ocean away to the west, are contained most of the creatures populating Lysenka II. The rest of the planet is almost entirely empty, except for indigenous spiders and a few winged insects. Don't forget that solar physicists and geognosticians tell us that this world is a very long way behind our worlds in development. Which is no doubt why it is the last refuge of capitalism."

There was some laughter at this sally. Although most of the tourists had no way of knowing what exactly capitalism was, the word had retained smutty connotations over the ages.

"That's the River Dunder we can see occasionally over to your left. It is not large as rivers on this planet go. On the other hemisphere is a river surveyed from the air which is almost twice as long as the River Amasonia on Earth. The Dunder flows over the ancient rift valley in which we now find ourselves. It is a river with many fish in the equivalent of an early Carboniferous Age development. The experts tell us that it is some 3,130 million years since Lysenka II become cool enough to allow the steam in the atmosphere to condense as rain. Now over to your right you can see if you turn your heads another grove of horsetails. Trees very like them once flourished on Earth."

"I think she plans to send us to sleep," Kordan said in a low voice to Sygiek.

"We can sleep at refreshment-time. Isn't this a fine road our people have built? We could conquer any planet in the galaxy."

"I have never entirely understood why we have not expanded our sphere of influence in space."

"'Utopia is an attitude, not a dimension,' if I may quote."

"All the same ... Of course, I don't question ..."

The superb road unwound before them, hour after hour. When it ran beside the River Dunder, more game was sighted, most of it fleeing for cover. The other three buses had disappeared into a tan distance which quivered in the noon heat.

Rubyna Constanza had taken a break from her commentary. Now she was back again, smiling prettily as before.

"You will have noticed many more animals beside the river. Mostly they catch fish, or they prey on those who catch fish. They are very clever at concealment. The brave system workers who built this road have tales to tell of their viciousness. Those workers and the soldiers who defended them were the only members of our people ever to be allowed weapons on Lysenka II—with the exception of the garrison that permanently defends Peace City, of course.

"As I expect you all understand," and she gave them a beautiful smile as reward for that understanding, "perhaps the most remarkable event in the entire history of Lysenka, from the point of view of *homo uniformis*, was the arrival here of a colony ship from Earth, 1.09 million years ago in the past, in bitter pre-utopian times on our home planet. In those far-off days, before our culture was established worldwide, and before the science of cratobatics was developed, fifty light years was a challengingly long distance. The colony ship was not heading for the Lysenkan system but for another system even farther away. However, something went wrong with the primitive drive, and the ship came down on this planet." She extended her hand forward, pointing through the front window. "It made a forced landing somewhere ahead there, not so many kilometers from the Dunderzee Gorge. That colony ship belonged to the now defunct *homo sapiens* capitalist system called America. It contained not less than—"

She stopped, gasping and staring through the window.

"Oh, sygygys! Look!"

Already most of the passengers were looking. There was an obstacle of some kind on the road ahead. As the bus plunged nearer, it could be seen that there was a slash right across the smooth surface, where the road had crinkled and collapsed.

The control systems of the bus were already automatically in operation. Its perceptions began to slow the heavy vehicle some milliseconds before the humans could respond. Brakes bit, squealing.

Momentum carried the bus forward toward the gap. Regentop flung herself into Takeido's arms. As the guide rushed shrieking toward the rear of the vehicle, Dulcifer grabbed her and held her close. Sygiek reached voluntarily for Kordan's arm. Some passengers screamed. Tires burned across the tarmac as the bus slewed sideways—and slid toward the obstruction.

The gap was no more than a meter and a half wide. The bus slid nearer, inertial systems bringing it almost to a halt. Then the front skirt went over the edge. The whole body tipped, teetered, and fell.

It crashed on to one shoulder, rolling till it settled on its side with a high rending sound. The passengers were flung into heaps along the right-hand side of the bus.

Dulcifer was among the first to recover. He saw that Constanza was unhurt and then began calling in a firm voice, saying that the danger was over and that everyone should climb out who could manage to do so. From the back of the bus, an older man, an underwater hydraulics technician called Lao Fererer, shouted out that he had the emergency exit open and would help anyone who needed help.

"My knee—it's so painful I don't dare move," gasped Kordan.

"Try," said Sygiek. She bit her bottom lip to stop it trembling.

One by one, helping and encouraging each other, the passengers climbed out. They gathered together on the road or sat dazedly on its verge. There was a little blood, but nobody was seriously hurt.

They looked about them, shocked by the unexpected accident, stunned by the heat outside the air-conditioned bus. Kordan, Lao Fererer and the woman with him, an interplanetary weather co-ordinator called Hete Orlon, and one or two other passengers, climbed to the upper side of the bus to gain a vantage point from which to survey the territory. It did not appear promising. Despite the great distances, the sunlight gave everything a cottony aspect, making seeing difficult and contributing to a dismal feeling of claustrophobia.

A thunderous silence reigned, punctuated by the ticking of the metal of the bus. A herd of two-legged animals, shaggy-maned and blunt of snout, gazed at them from a distance of a hundred meters. All stood in more or less identical poses of alertness. In the river, things swam, turning their seal-like heads toward the scene of the crash. Everything waited. Movement hung suspended in the damp, leathery air.

"Welcome to Lysenka II," said Ian Takeido. He laughed, but nobody else did.

IV

Kordan climbed down to stand with sober face beside Sygiek. The ongoing nature of a land vehicle; the whisper of air-conditioning; the long-familiar experience of hearing a voice electronically transmitted; listening to mildly tedious lectures; promise of an hospitable destination; all those things had vanished which, while they existed, had shielded the tourists from the understanding that they were but specks on an alien face, a long way from the System, vulnerable.

Rubyna Constanza brushed down her red uniform and said, with a tolerable imitation of her official voice, "Please do not stray too far from the bus. There is no cause for alarm. We shall be missed when we do not rendezvous at the Gorge with the other buses. Although the radio is not working, they can phone to Unity by land-line, and Air Rescue will come out immediately." As an afterthought, she added, "Normally, the bus itself is in constant radio contact with Unity . . ."

"How many E-hours is all that going to take?" asked a fair-haired woman, a seasons technician with great experience of the Saturn micro-system. "It will be dark in another seven hours, won't it? What happens if no one has arrived by then?"

"We've still eight or nine hours of daylight, haven't we?" another voice asked.

These questions were never answered.

A row of dark heads appeared over the roadside embankment. Heads and shoulders, eyes, low brows. Scrutinizing the group of tourists. Regarding the wrecked bus. Nobody moved. Metal crackled.

Those dark heads and withered unimaginable faces had such a petrifying effect on the tourists that tides of time seemed to drift by like the clouds overhead. Then one of the animals hopped up from the bank and stood alertly on the highway. It took another leap, bringing it almost under the trailing skirt of the LDB. It curled back its lips and showed grey teeth.

The tourists shrank away, closing ranks. They were confronting something which filled them with an overwhelming sense of dread. The unknown had hitherto formed no part of their existence; everything that was regimented and comfortable quailed before this demon. Its darting gaze, its stance, challenged the rules they lived by.

"Look . . ." began Kordan. But he had nothing to say.

The animal was 1.5 meters high. It remained where it was, in a crouch, content, master of the situation. Two of its fellows scrambled up the bank and joined it, standing slightly in its rear. The three of them waited, teeth bared, snouts twitching. The tourists could hear their continual sniffing, and the rasp of their nails on the road surface.

Roughly human-shaped, the animals possessed disproportionately long arms and large paddle-like front paws, which hung to the ground. Their feet were flat and almost round, and studded with calluses. The faces were startling, the sandy flesh contorted into whorls; the effect was of a cross between man and mole, with deep-sunk little eyes set behind an armored nose, and bristling hair covering most of the skull. The bodies were covered with patchy fur.

Hete Orlon began to sob.

"The Id!" exclaimed Takeido, not without relish.

Far from showing fear, the mole-creatures evinced signs which could be interpreted as eagerness to get at the tourists if only they knew how. The tourists watched as more creatures came swarming up the embankment. A dozen of them climbed nimbly up, to stand behind their leader. Their confidence was growing. They dared to look away from the tourists, grunting to each other and licking their furry lips.

Some sort of decision was arrived at between them. The leading mole-creature took a step forward, raising a paw at the same time. As he did so, a well-aimed boot struck him squarely in the muzzle.

With a cry, the creature clutched at his face. Blood burst from under his paw. He swung round, blundering among his companions. With one accord, they all turned. With one accord, they all ran, jumped and fled down the bank. In a moment, they were gone. The cottony landscape appeared deserted again.

Vul Dulcifer walked forward and retrieved his boot. He sat on the grey road surface, pulling it on methodically. His rough features betrayed no expression.

The tourists found their tongues again. The spell was broken.

They spread out across the road, peering anxiously through the thick light, arguing amongst themselves as to whether Dulcifer's violent action was justified. Had the animals been merely curious?

"It was a moment for individual action, comrades, not a committee meeting," said Dulcifer. He remained sitting in the road, looking at them.

Among the party was a general purposes doctor, a silent man called Lech Czwartek, who was noticeable because he alone of the party wore a small goatee beard. He spoke now, addressing his remark to Dulcifer.

"You realize that you have now convinced those animals that we are hostile?"

Unmoved, Dulcifer said, "We *are* hostile."

However debatable Dulcifer's action, the group felt encouraged. Some of them climbed back on the side of the bus. Others stood on the bank, watching for signs of movement.

Kordan raised his arms and said in a commanding voice, "Listen to me. It is best that we form a leadership group to co-ordinate action. We should debate whether to set fire to the bus, in order to keep off the beasts until help arrives."

"There's food and drink and shelter in the bus," protested one woman, a dark-faced unionist leader from Mercury Second Station.

"We'll need to sleep in it tonight, if help does not arrive," said another.

"That's defeatist talk," said a third.

"Speak according to the rules of debate," said Kordan. "You will all get your chance. Sygiek 194 and I will hear all your points in turn, then we decide on a co-ordinated line of action. We must remain organized . . . Unity Breeds Immunity."

In the long debate that followed, everyone stated his point of view, some timidly, some defiantly. From all this, Dulcifer stood aside, arms akimbo, looking toward the river. Leaving the group about Kordan, Sygiek went over to him and said, "You are sensibly watching for danger, Vul Dulcifer. We should post look-outs before talking. The next pack of beasts may prove less timid than the last."

"There are only so many boots to go round."

"It is questionable wisdom to allow wild beasts on a planet with innocent holiday-makers."

"It's their planet."

"Not any more."

"Millia Sygiek, while your friend Kordan is making his speeches, I want to go down this embankment and look around. My belief is that these mole-like creatures undermined the road and wrecked our bus."

"Deliberately?"

"That we may be able to establish. Come down with me and see."

The embankment was steep. He ran down, digging his heels in as he went. As she followed him, and they slithered down to the level of the nearby river, Kordan called her name. She did not look back.

Kordan came to the edge of the highway and called, "Where are you two going? We must not split up. Remain united!"

She followed Dulcifer. She wondered if something in his stocky figure, his air of confidence, reminded her of the director of the crèche in which, with a thousand other infants, she had spent the tender years of infancy, following her exobirth.

Under the low cliffs where the river had once flowed, the land was strewn with debris. Here and there, the terrain had been built up into long winding tunnels, standing over a meter high. It was hard to determine whether these odd features were natural or artificial. Between the tunnels and on top of them grew fleshy ferns which sprayed rusty spores into the air as Dulcifer and Sygiek brushed past. Several tunnels led under the embankment on which the road was built.

Dulcifer kicked at the soil. "Here's where the road collapsed. There's no doubt in my mind that these tunnels are made by the mole-like animals. They would be safe in their tunnels from most other predators. They burrowed under the road and the freeway collapsed—presumably by accident, not from intent. Depends how intelligent they are. All the same . . ."

He noticed her expression. "You're looking upset. What's the trouble?"

She drew herself up. "Utopianist Dulcifer, I have observed how free you are at expressing opinions. You hold an ill-concealed contempt for democratic consensus opinion, that's obvious. Then you casually order me to follow you here, as if I were some inferior—an ateptotic from Centauri, say. In my judgment, you are at least a potential deviationist, and I advise you to keep a check on your behavior."

While he stared at her, a bead of sweat ran down his brow, into his eyelashes, distorting the image of her. As he cleared his eye with a finger, he said, "Or else you'll put in a report, eh? I did not order you down here. You followed me."

"We are not supposed to split up."

"Let's forget it and concentrate on real problems." He took a step toward her. "You're bossy but you are no fool, Sygiek. We can be attacked at any time, once these foul creatures get used to us and realize we are not a menace. By attacked, I mean attacked, overcome and eaten, you understand. The question is, what do we do? I wanted to see—"

"Hey, you two!" The Moscow bureaucrat, Georg Morits, was scrambling down the embankment toward them, his figure outlined against the tan sky. They faced him as he slithered to a halt and wagged a finger at them. "Aren't you forgetting some elementary rules? 'Action is corporate . . .' We are setting up an action committee, and we require that you both return to the LDB at once."

Dulcifer made a move toward him, and Morits backed against one of the tunnels.

"Don't chant slogans at me, fellow. I don't sit on my arse in a Moscow office all day. Survival is not to be had through mouthing dogma. I'll come when I'm ready. Tell Kordan that."

Morits pressed himself against the tunnel wall, saying weakly, "Don't attack me for what was a unanimous decision. There are unknown dangers here and the—uh-uh-uh-uh-uh- . . ."

As his voice failed, his face went ashen. His body seemed to shrivel. He staggered but could not fall. A cry almost like a solid thing was torn from his throat.

Rushing to take hold of him, Sygiek and Dulcifer saw sharp claws and leathery paws grasping the bureaucrat's thighs, biting deep into his flesh until blood seeped across his clothes. Those terrible hands had struck at him through the wall of the tunnel from behind. Had Morits been sitting there, the claws would have struck his throat and he would already be dead.

Calling loudly for assistance, the two utopians seized Morits's arms and tried to drag him forward. He uttered another desolate scream. As they pulled him slowly away, part of the tunnel wall behind him collapsed. Amid falling sand milled several of the mole-creatures. Their trap had been sprung and they were still clasping their prey. Their muzzles were bloodied. Morits was already being devoured.

For a moment they crouched at the hole, as if contemplating an attack. Other faces appeared in the gap, sniffing.

Dulcifer let go his hold on Morits and kicked out, catching a bristling flank with his boot.

"Stand back!" Sygiek ordered. She pulled a small gun out of her tunic. Dulcifer barely had time to duck before she straightened her arm and fired two shots in a professional manner into the hole.

The gun was hetrasonic. Even as two buzzing notes sounded, two of the mole-creatures fell forward, clutching their bellies as they went. Writhing, they dropped to the ground, but hardly were they there before their fellows had taken them, dragging them into the tunnel. Bellowing, Dulcifer rushed forward and grabbed one of the wounded creatures, wrenching it away from its fellows, kicking out to fend off another attack. The rabble had had enough. Holding the other wounded creature, they retreated into the hole and disappeared from view.

Dulcifer and Sygiek turned and stared at each other. Both were pale. Dulcifer dashed sweat from his brow.

"You are not permitted to carry a gun," he panted. "System legality and so on."

She said, "I have a license."

He wiped at the sweat again and looked stupidly down at the ground. He required no more explanation. Millia Sygiek was a member of the dreaded USRP, and Reason Police were authorized to carry weapons and fire when necessary.

"So you hunt with that pack," he said heavily. "I'm sorry to hear it. I took you for a decent woman."

The tourist party on the embankment had heard the scuffle. Some of them were already hurrying down to help. Dulcifer stood back and let them. He retained his hold on the mole-creature which Sygiek had shot; it was now dead. He followed as the others tenderly carried Morits up to the road and into the shade of the overturned bus. A trail of blood dripped from the wounded bureaucrat.

Kordan and the grey-haired hydraulics technician, Lao Fererer, had established themselves as provisional co-directors of the party. They cleared a space for the bodies and called for bandages.

The guide, Rubyna Constanza, climbed into the bus, reappearing with bandages and medicaments. She set to work in a business-like way to tend Morits, kneeling by him and turning him gently over on his face. Then she cried aloud. Morits's clothing, the small of his back, his buttocks, thighs, calves, part of one arm, had been eaten away as if by rats, exposing bone. Blood was seeping over the road. Mercifully, Morits was unconscious.

Constanza looked up into the tense faces round her.

"What can we do about his wounds here? He will surely die. In the Unity, at Peace City, the accident units could grow replacement arteries and flesh but here . . . Death's certain."

Nobody spoke. It was the obscene word "death" which shocked them. At home, there was only a fulfilled Passing On, as the citizen moved into an all-embracing pallor which was in harmony with the system. Here on Lysenka II, you went out in crimson, the hue of rage and passion.

Kordan spoke, mastering his voice. "Do what you can for him, Rubyna Constanza. Now we see why we are inevitably screened before we can visit an Extra-solar Planet. Instead of Eternal Security, we are faced with Eternal Anarchy. In the System, before the days of Biocom and the establishment of World Unity—"

"We already have the speeches by heart," Sygiek cut in. "It is not an hour since this vehicle crashed and already one of us is severely wounded. Danger surrounds us, and our first duty to the state is to triumph over that danger and survive. All of you make sure you now understand exactly the situation in which we find ourselves. Ecologically and ideologically, these creatures are our enemies." Her arm swept round to cover the wilderness about them. "We are Number One Target for every living monster out there."

Dragging the dead mole-creature by its mane of hair, Dulcifer pushed his way into the center of the group. He dumped it beside the bleeding body of Georg Morits.

"Sygiek is right. We don't want speeches, we want action. We don't want propaganda, we want information. We aren't in Utopia now. You know what permits Utopia to flourish? I'll tell you—protein. A plentiful supply of protein, eh? The one prime fact about Lysenka you'd better remember is that from the word go it suffered from protein-deficiency on a grand scale. Know what that means, comrades? *We can be eaten.* To the things that exist here, we are protein on the hoof, and we have to fight. Otherwise, we'll be more thoroughly chewed up and gulped down something's digestive tract than even poor Comrade Morits."

V

A murmur of shock and protest rose from the stranded tourists, but Dulcifer pushed on through it.

"We may be efficient in the System, but we have had no external enemies for countless centuries. Here, we are inefficient. On this dud, murderous world, we are just bait. Food, nothing more. We need knowledge and leadership to survive for even a few hours."

"Collective leadership," said Lao Fererer, to a murmur of agreement. "We have lived by our principles—we are certainly not going to abandon them in a crisis."

"We adapt," Dulcifer said firmly. "Lysenka II is just entering what corresponds with the start of Earth's Carboniferous Age, hundreds of millions of years ago. We are as good as stuck in the past, long before Biocom was thought of. We need to understand that situation as clearly as possible. Rubyna Constanza, you're the guide—give us a quick summary of planetary conditions as we have to face them in this Rift Valley."

Constanza had finished bandaging the badly wounded man. She rose to her feet and faced them. After a swift glance at Kordan, the Outourist girl spoke as if still delivering an address on her consigned vehicle.

"The evidence for Lysenka's having just emerged from a Devonian Age is complex, and has much to do with the state of the local sun. But geological and biobotanical evidence reinforce a general picture. Essentially, we have here a world of primitive life. In the oceans are fish some meters long with bony head armor. Also trilobites. System scientists have discovered bones of tetrapod amphibians in this valley which resemble a terrestrial rhipidistian order. That is to say, not fossil bones—the creatures existed recently but were all eaten by the invaders. In other parts of the planet, toward the tropics, they still exist, haunting the shores of the Borodinian Lakes.

"The plant life is of a matching antiquity, as we would expect. You may see dragonflies of up to seventy centimeters' wing span. They are becoming extinct because their larvae in the rivers are regarded by the animals as a delicacy. They lived particularly in the swamp region to the west of this road, where there are forests of giant-scale trees. Such forests are more frequent near the equator. Here you will mostly find cage trees, horsetails, calamites, maybe some gingkoes, and of course fern trees and fern, with no seed-bearing plants. There are no flowers on Lysenka II, a fact which some of our visitors have complained about. There are also giant sequoias, bearing their stiff wooden flowers or cones.

"Thus we see that the only brains on the planet are dim and instinct-driven. No creature at all resembling mankind could possibly have emerged for millions of years, if it had not been for the capitalist ship which crash-landed in this region so long ago."

The tourists had listened attentively if anxiously to all this. Running a hand through his sandy hair, Takeido said, "Yes, I would like to amplify briefly what Rubyna Constanza has been saying. I am an exobotanist with five years' field-work on the planet Sokolev. As Constanza implies, here on Lysenka nature has yet to invent the angiosperm. That's seeds in an encased ovary, the opposite of gymnosperms. An angiosperm is a nutritious little food-package which supports seeds in the primary stage of their life. Spores or unpackaged seeds have no such advantage—they fend for themselves and their mortality rate is high. You can't eat spores. But angiosperms—those little food-packages are what caused the first proliferation of mammals over the face of Earth. They can make a world get up and go. So this world is a non-starter—as yet, at least. Thank you."

"As for the question of grass," began Regentop, but Dulcifer cut her off.

"That's the essence of it. There are no grasses on this world, no cereals, no high-energy packets for animals to eat—no basic requisite for the support of a grazer-predator system such as grew up on Earth and Sokolev and elsewhere. Lysenka has not yet reached a stage where it can naturally support anything called animal life."

"You talk a great deal, Utopianist Dulcifer," said Fererer, and pointed to the dead mole-creature, "but this animal you brought here—"

"You should not lead even a sedentary committee," said Dulcifer, pointing a finger at Fererer, "if you have not grasped the salient point that there was reason for our being screened before we were allowed on Lysenka II. This is not an animal. There are no real animals on Lysenka II. The whole grazer-predator system is *human* in origin."

With his toecap, he rolled the mud-covered tunneler over until it sprawled on its back with its wound visible, one arm stretched across the road, one limp across its chest.

"Look at it, Fererer, and you others. Look and feel pity. See its retractable genitals, its joints, its anatomical structure. It is made what it is by harsh conditioning. It is just a poor savage misfit. This is what it has been reduced to, generation by generation. But its ancestors were our ancestors. They were human, *homo sapiens,* a poor confused race that blundered around until it found the stars. Same goes for every damned animal we are likely to encounter in this valley. They're ex-human stock. That's the danger we have to understand. We are up against—not instinct, but cunning."

It was the statement, "Its ancestors were our ancestors," which provoked the biggest murmur. Sygiek's voice cut through their comments.

"Utopianist Dulcifer, I hereby give you notice that you will be reported for deviationism on our return to Unity. You waste valuable time, and you discuss Classified information before someone who is not a member of the élite."

"But the guide *knows*," exclaimed a ferrous metal analyst called Che Burek. "She knows, she lives here, she's been indoctrinated."

"She is still only a guide, a worker," said Sygiek. "No offense, Comrade Constanza. Except for Fererer, we did not need reminding that all Lysenkan animals claim descent from the capitalists who crashed here. Of course there are dangers; but the fact that the animals are semi-human will enable us to use the system's most powerful weapon —*reason!*"

Dulcifer uttered a dry laugh and kicked the corpse so that it rolled against the chassis of the bus.

"That comes well from you, Sygiek! You should know better. You shot this thing."

"Retract, Sygiek," called Che Burek.

"Enough. No indulging in personalities," said Kordan, stepping forward. "More than one of us is capable of making reports. We understand our position, don't we? The bus log tells us that we are approximately two hundred and fifty kilometers out from the Unity Hotel. Six hours of daylight remain. We have emergency flares and torches and other equipment in the vehicle, also a trolley which will carry supplies. We are now going to march in a body back to the safety of our hotel. The likelihood of attack on the road is remote."

Usla Denning, a woman from the Cupran State who was accompanying Che Burek, said, "Such a walk will take us over two E-days, without allowing for rest periods. That means a Lysenkan day and a half. And by the way, I'm one of the System's leading seasons technicians, and I believe a storm is brewing."

"We have made our decision," said Kordan and Fererer together.

"May I put forward an alternative, although I am only a worker?" asked Constanza. She was a slight, trim figure, and she regarded them almost with an amused air. "Unity is a stiff uphill march, and I presume none of you is used to walking far. There is a nearer refuge, and it lies downhill. At the Gorge itself is a comfortable restaurant with plenty of restrooms, saunas, and so on, plus a swimming pool in part of the lake especially for your convenience."

"How far away is the Gorge?" asked a dozen voices.

"Under an hour's LDB travel. Say one hundred and

eighty, one hundred and eighty-five kilometers. We shall be safe at the Gorge."

They held an impromptu discussion.

While they were talking, a distant note of a horn was heard.

"A vehicle!" someone exclaimed, and they all ran to look up and down the road. One or two of them climbed on the bus.

The freeway lay empty in both directions, fading into dun-colored haze. They were completely isolated from civilization. To one side, perhaps a kilometer away, the plain ended and an old green forest began. A herd of creatures was issuing from the trees and coming at a brisk gait toward the embankment and the river that lay between forest and embankment. In the thick light, it was impossible to distinguish their characteristics clearly.

Everyone stood and watched.

"I'll get those emergency flares," said Che Burek, but he made no move.

The herd comprised perhaps fifty individuals. They progressed with a lolloping gait, and seemingly on all fours. At the rear were three runners proceeding with a more upright stance. One of these three raised an instrument to his mouth and blew a ragged note. This was the horn they had heard.

The sound of it—unpleasantly reminiscent of a huntsman's horn—was enough to promote terror among the tourists. Without waiting to form a committee, they climbed into the bus, scrambling through doors and windows. Only Kordan, Takeido and Dulcifer were left standing on the road.

"Assist me in getting Georg Morits into the coach," said Kordan to Dulcifer, going over to the wounded man.

Together the three of them heaved Morits up the slope of the cab, where other hands helped lift him inside as gently as possible.

At this juncture, Morits roused from his coma, struggled and started feebly screaming. His bandages began to ooze. He waved his arm in pain, smearing blood everywhere. A convulsion seized his entire body, he arched himself backward, cried again, collapsed. Lech Czwartek, the doctor, was by his side; after examination, he shook his head and pronounced Morits dead.

Hardly were the words out of his mouth than Hete Orlon went into an hysterical fit. She threw herself about, tore her hair, and struck at Lao Fererer as he tried to comfort her. Then she hurled herself weeping on the dead body, crying incoherently.

"Mother, mother, what have I done to you? They have taken all your beads away. It's not for me and not for you. No one's to blame, mother, no one's to blame, I swear—not me, not you! Why did you ever leave me? We're both safe together, little mother!"

Fererer put his arms round her heaving shoulders, trying to comfort her. Turning a red face to the others, he said, "I don't know what she is saying. I can assure you she was an exobirth, like the rest of us. She had no mother. She was brought up in a crèche with her other siblings in Mali Zemlya."

While Orlon subsided into troubled gasps, the creatures from the forest were drawing closer. They took their time, swinging along between the sparse green fronds, looking perpetually to left and to right.

Their features were not more clearly distinguishable. They were brown-and-white striped. Their ears were remarkably large and round, and cupped forward almost as if they formed extensions to the lower jaw.

"They look like zebras," said Dennig, in a relieved voice. "Could they be grazers, rather than carnivores?"

The herd slowed, skirting some mole tunnels. They approached the river with due caution. Occasionally they stopped entirely, raising their front feet off the ground to look round in a man-like stance. The tourists were fascinated.

"To imagine that they were once human . . ." exclaimed Lydy Fracx.

"To think that they were once capitalists," said Kordan.

"To think that they are born inside the female still," said Takeido. "Only when Biocom delivered our kind from that burden could the familial societies be dismantled and a true global society established."

"Quiet!" said Sygiek.

The striped herd had seen the bus. They looked at it

for a long time and then moved toward the river. Wide stretches of sand on either side of the water showed how the river had shrunk from its original state; but it was still considerable and looked treacherous, with boulders rising above its rolling surface here and there, and a channel in the middle where the race was deep, sending up a mane of foam which seemed to run perpetually before a silent wind.

The leaders of the zebras plunged into the water and the rest followed. One of the rear runners blew his horn again like a challenge. Females and younger members of the group were positioned protectively inside a circle of pressing bodies as they braved the flood. The leaders had reached the deeper water when they were attacked. A tough gray-maned male suddenly fell to his knees and almost disappeared beneath threshing water. Two of his companions grabbed him with their forefeet and pulled him up. A dark-bodied seal-creature came up with him, its fangs sunk into his belly. It was immediately attacked by the other zebra-people.

More of the seals appeared. General confusion ensued, in which more than one of the younger zebras was hauled screaming beneath the flood. The first seal was dispatched with a stunning blow. It lost its grip and was carried rapidly downstream. Something grey and fast had it almost at once, and it disappeared from sight.

The zebra herd milled and plunged about. It had backed into shallower water. The horn was blown again; as it was raised in the air to sound three tipsy notes, the watchers saw its elaborate design. Afterward, they were to argue whether it was fashioned from bone, wood, or metal.

Those brazen notes rallied the indecisive creatures. Wheeling, they moved back to the far bank in good order. Without once looking back at the spot where several among them had been lost, they moved along the top of the cliff with that all-fours gait until they grew small in the distance.

"We could have driven them off easily, if it had come to it," said Kordan breezily. "Now, let us gather supplies together and prepare to walk down to the Gorge as soon as we can."

"I have just remembered something important," said Jaini Regentop. "Every ten kilometers or so along the road,

51

there are landphones. Presumably it was a system installed for the convenience of the road-builders. I observed the phones from the bus. We can walk to the nearest one and phone for help."

"Why didn't you have the sense to mention this before?" asked Takeido.

"Why didn't the guide mention it? She has seen those phones over and over again."

"I had forgotten," said Constanza, snapping her fingers. "I have never known anyone have occasion to use those phones. Besides, I'm only a stupid worker, aren't I?"

"We have occasion to use the phones now!" said Kordan. "Our plan of action is clear. No more delay. We walk toward the Gorge and stop at the nearest landphone. If it works, we summon help. Then it may be best to return here to the bus and wait—"

"And find it already overrun by ferocious animals!" exclaimed Hete Orlon, who was still looking tearful. "I am not leaving the safety of this bus, whatever the rest of you decide."

Ignoring the interruption, Kordan continued, "If the phone doesn't work, we carry on toward the Gorge. Rubyna Constanza has told us that it is only one hundred and eighty kilometers. She also informs me that a routine maintenance crew patrols the road from Peace City at dawn every morning, so relief will be on its way, even if we cannot get through by landphone—and even if one of the tourist buses does not drive back from the Gorge to find what has happened to us. Is this all agreed? May we have a show of hands, comrades."

Disagreement immediately broke out. What should be done about Orlon? Others besides her did not want to leave the bus. Would not a big group on the road be a target for attack?

It took half an E-hour to decide that a small party of six with provisions would go forward. The rest would stay by the bus.

"Who has to go in this small party?" asked Czwartek, anxiously scratching his beard. "As a doctor, my duty is to stay here with the larger party."

"It is a privilege to go forward, Utopianist Doctor," cried Sygiek, flinging up her hand. "I shall go with my partner, Jerezy Kordan. Fererer will remain here in charge of the bus party, and to look after poor feeble creatures like Orlon. Volunteers to go with Kordan and me to assemble here in a line. We want no cowards, either—this is a miserable backward capitalist planet for which we should feel every contempt."

Several volunteers stepped forward, among them the burly Dulcifer.

"Utopianist Dulcifer, you are under criticism," said Sygiek. "You will remain with the bus."

Kordan touched her arm. "You must not give all the orders," he said. "Dulcifer is a resourceful man, even if he is from Venus. Let him come in our party—we can then keep him under surveillance. That is best."

After some further argument, the six were agreed upon. Besides Sygiek, Kordan and Dulcifer, the party was to consist of Rubyna Constanza and the two young men from different sectors of the Martian State, Ian Takeido, the exobotanist, and Che Burek, the metals analyst. Takeido's partner, Regentop, was to have gone, but she and Takeido quarreled, so that Burek stepped into her place. He was a well-built cheerful man who announced that he would be pleased to take orders.

VI

The six set off, waving farewell and giving the System salute. They took with them a motorized luggage truck which had been stowed in the rear compartment of the bus. On this were loaded provisions, flares and other items. They marched sturdily down the center of the freeway, in single file with the truck in their midst. The bus was left behind and obscured by a slow curve in the road. They were alone in the immense tan landscape. Silence dwelt over them.

A breeze rose and died. An immense dragonfly came to inspect them, hovering above them for some way. The river meandered away from the road. The land became more uneven. They remained in the center of a great inverted bowl of soupy air. Only once did the sun shine through the cloud sufficiently to be remarked as a blurry disk.

An E-hour and a half had passed before they saw the post of a landphone in the distance. By it stood a large road sign. As the party approached, the letters on the sign formed themselves into words:

DUNDERZEE GORGE 200 Km.

Work—Enjoy—Learn Even From Scenery

"Oh, it's much farther than I remembered," Constanza exclaimed. "This journey is so fast and easy by LDB."

55

"We're certainly learning more than we want from this damned scenery," said Dulcifer.

"Just recall that the magnificent road on which we walk is a part of our culture," said Kordan.

When they reached the phone, it was Sygiek who opened the armored box and switched on. The others stood by the trolley, looking on expectantly. The small screen did not light.

"Defunct," she said. She switched off and closed the box. Takeido pushed her aside and tried himself, joggling the switch up and down, without result.

"So much for our culture," he said. He looked half-regretfully at Kordan. "We'll never make the Gorge. You and I will never have our confidential discussion. These —these protein-seekers will have us as soon as the sun goes down." He hopped on top of the luggage truck and began to whistle.

Kordan cleared his throat, frowned at the younger man, then stared up at the low clouds overhead.

They stood there forlornly under the big sign, avoiding each other's gaze.

"Can we go back to the bus?" asked Constanza. "I know it sounds decadent, but my shoes are pinching my feet."

"Walk without your shoes," said Sygiek, curtly. "We must strike on to the next phone and the one after that, if necessary. It's no good giving up, comrades. Let's keep some good utopianist hope in our hearts."

"And what should we keep in our heads?" asked Burek. Shaking his head, he said to Sygiek, "You and Kordan talk so much. Blowing never warmed porridge, as the old country saying has it." He gave the impression of a withdrawn man, which made his remarks the more effective, especially as he spoke in a slow heavy way, drawing his brows together as he did so. "My friends, we must suppose that the tunnelers ripped out the phone-cables back by the coach. So no phones are going to work all the way to the Gorge, are they? Use your brains."

"Exactly so. That's another reason for getting back to the bus," said Constanza.

"It may be an excuse but it is not a reason," said Burek. "I am myself for continuing. I merely do not want us to

56

suffer disappointment every time we reach a phone and find it out of order."

"Let me remind you that our decision was to make for the Gorge," said Kordan. "The others rely on us to carry out our intention. We should inevitably be criticized if we went back having achieved nothing."

"That's up to them," said Takeido, sliding off the truck. "I'd rather be criticized then eaten. Not that I can bear either." He clutched his forehead in sudden tension. "I wish I had never heard of Lysenka II! Listen, if we walked back to the phone post situated *before* that fatal bit of tunneling, we should find the line working."

"Why didn't you suggest that at the bus?" wailed Constanza.

He took her hand. "Because it has only just occurred to me, of course, you lovely creature."

Dulcifer burst out laughing.

"What do you find amusing?" Burek asked him. "Are you for going on or back?"

"There's something in what Takeido says. Better disgrace than digestion. I am for going back."

"How typical of you," said Sygiek. "Anything to be difficult. That makes three wishing to go on and three wishing to go back. Do we split up again into two parties?"

"Let's just have a rest," said Constanza. She sank to the ground, and Takeido sat companionably beside her. In the argument that followed, she played no part; her bare feet spoke tenderly for her. The other four stood solidly on the road, debating and looking across the bleak landscape.

They were still arguing when Sygiek burst out, "You spineless people, you have sore feet but no spirit! The Gorge it must be. We can walk throughout the night, using torches and flares to ward off attack. I will go forward alone if necessary."

At which Dulcifer nodded, smiling, and gave her a round of silent applause.

"It's not a matter of spirit but of understanding the situation," said Burek, drawing his brows together. "The six of us would be no match for an attack by thirty or forty of these creatures. Our duty is to recognize realities and return to the main party to acquaint them with the situation. You wish to go on from personal reasons, Millia

Sygiek, because you are a person keen to dominate others and subject them to your will. Jerezy Kordan wishes to go on, not because he is strong but because he is weak and wishes to please you. Set your personality aside and see sense, utopianist."

Dulcifer clapped Burek on the back and gave a bark of laughter.

Burek looked at him steadily. "You are as much subject to your personal desires as they," he said. "And you are more to blame because you have more understanding."

Breaking from his silence, Kordan said, "No more rustic opinions, please, Che Burek. Remember we are all utopianists and derive our strength through unity. We have no decision to make—we will go forward as already decided."

Takeido gave a low whistle, "Comrades, the ex-capitalists are beginning to take an interest in us once more." He stood up and pointed through the thick atmosphere.

Down from the road, across a wearying jumble of rocks and canyons studded with horsetails, their gaze traveled, searching the brown wilderness until their eyes lit on a group of figures crouching on a prominence and surveying them.

As if they had waited to be seen, the distant figures rose and began to climb slowly down in single file.

"Not many of them," observed Kordan. "Stupid of us not to bring binoculars along. We will continue to walk on at a steady pace. No cause for alarm."

Taking hold of the luggage trolley, he set the example. Sygiek fell in beside him, Burek and Dulcifer followed. Takeido helped Constanza to her feet and they walked behind the others, Takeido keeping hold of the guide's hand.

Without undue haste, the indistinct figures of the enemy scrambled down to the floor of the rift valley and moved toward the road, closing in as the minutes passed. It was clear that the utopians were their target.

As the trolley growled before them over the road, Sygiek said quietly to Kordan, "Do you notice they seem to have two heads? Oh, I feel such horror—less fear than horror. Surely they were never of *homo sapiens* stock? Shall we commence running?"

"If we run, so will they. My knowledge of history tells

me that it might make better sense to fire off some flares and try to scare them away. Allow me to say that I fear more for your safety than for mine. Dearest Millia, what should we do?"

She looked at him and smiled tensely. "I will back whatever you do."

He flashed her a grateful look. "Let's try to drive these monsters off."

The six stopped in the middle of the road and drew together. A case of flare-guns was broken open; armed, they turned to face the creatures now rapidly approaching across the barren valley.

The enemy halted. It consisted of five ferocious individuals, each looking more formidable than any life-form the tourists had seen so far. Each wore a kind of coat of short, bristling spines. Each had a face painted with drab vertical stripes; two black horizontal stripes partly masked the eyes. Each had hair which piled up stiffly like a cock's-comb above its head. They resembled enormous perambulating cacti.

The exception was the leader, who halted ahead of his four companions. A bone with sharply spiked ends pierced the flanges of his nostrils. On his head, above a mass of unruly yellow hair, he carried a skull like a crown, the teeth of its upper jaw biting into his forehead. The skull was painted in similar patterns to his face. It was this skull that, in a moment of fear, had made Sygiek think the newcomers were two-headed.

They were mounted on steeds, carrying spears and sitting erect. In their watchful silence, they were extremely menacing. Despite their extraordinary garb, they bore more definitely than any other creature encountered on Lysenka the stamp of humanity.

"Terrifying," said Takeido. He clutched his mouth with his hand.

"Do we or don't we use the flare-guns?" demanded Constanza, in an urgent whisper. "If we had just one good gun, we could wipe them all out." She clung to Takeido.

"When I give the signal, fire into their faces," said Sygiek. "And not until I give the signal, understand?"

The hunters were dismounting. Their steeds, their debased two-legged horses, were zebra-creatures, similar to the ones which had attempted unsuccessfully to cross the river. They carried the hunters piggy-back. Narrow saddles were secured just above their rumps. Spiked stirrups hung to their knees. When their riders dismounted, the five zebras fell to the ground, showing every sign of exhaustion, and took no further interest in the proceedings.

The five hunters stepped forward, bristling in their strange armor. They held their spears at the ready. The leader grunted a word of command, never lifting his scrutiny from the tourists standing on the road above him. One of his men turned in leisurely fashion, lifted his fingers to his painted lips, and whistled. Two notes. Pause. Then the two notes repeated.

The landscape filled with dogs. Yapping shrilly, they rose from the ground on all sides, a ferocious hunting pack. Their coats were stiff and bristling like those of their masters. Some of them had faces like wolves, some were blunt-faced and more human. Some ran only on four legs, some went sometimes on two. All converged on the party at bay on the road.

Within seconds, the tourists were surrounded.

"Flares?" asked Dulcifer. "I'll shoot the first hound to nip my ankles."

"Wait," said Burek. "They're not attacking us."

The leader of the hunters moved forward, striding through the snarling pack. He jumped effortlessly on to the road and confronted the tourists, standing as solid as a great barrel. He pointed at them and spoke.

The series of guttural noises he made was rapid and without meaning for them. They cringed before him until Kordan took a deep breath and stepped forward.

"We are people of importance," Kordan told him. "World Unity and the System are behind us. We demand that you help us return to Unity Hotel. Understand?"

"You're welcome to your stinking planet," shouted Takeido, when the other made no sign. "We just want to get home."

Sygiek held out her hand. In it was a packet of bread rolls with vegetable filling, made up by the hotel that morning. She offered it to the chief.

"A gift," she said. "You take it, you aid us."

The hunter chief turned, came close, and regarded her, ignoring her outstretched hand to stare into her eyes.

A strong psychic shock overcame her as her gaze met his. He was lean, arrogant, ruthless; those characteristics beamed from his attitude, from his narrow eyes. And some other quality that she had never met before, some mysterious mainspring of life which assaulted her, before which she felt humble. Of that unwanted humility she was ashamed; but she dropped her eyes submissively before his slitted gaze.

He snatched the bread package and hurled it to the dogs. Constanza clutched Takeido, who put an arm protectively round her. Seeing the movement, the leader flicked his head round and glared at them. Then he made an imperious gesture which there was no mistaking. They were to follow him.

From his henchman came more whistles. Additional hunters appeared from cover. They leaped on zebra-creatures and galloped forward, often accompanied by dogs. Yelping with excitement, they poured up to the road and overran it. The tourists were surrounded by milling men and hounds. Other warriors kept appearing.

More imperious gestures, more snarled commands.

"We have no choice but—" began Kordan, pale of face, when Takeido fired his flare-gun at the chief hunter.

The range was less than four meters. The chief had half-turned to summon his companions. The flare struck his shoulder and exploded, sending him tumbling among his hounds. Showers of green light burst among the wolf-pack. Snarling creatures fled in all directions.

"Everyone fire," cried Sygiek. "It's our only chance." Her flare-gun exploded as she spoke. Her five comrades followed her example.

Green dazzle filled the dun world. Several hunters fell, some ran away, the zebras galloped about shrieking. It made no difference. Fresh hunters materialized from the barren ground. They hurled themselves on the tourists and bore them to the ground by force. This was accompanied by savage yelling, intimidating in itself.

Bruised and frightened, disarmed, the tourists lay where they had been thrown. Hunters and dogs executed an angry parade round them, stamping spears or feet against the road surface. The tourists were able to make an unpleasantly close inspection of the hounds as they milled by.

Some of the dogs were dogs, snapping or jumping over one another. Some of them were children of the hunters, running on all fours like real hounds. Dogs and children alike were buttoned into the same type of bristling protective coat the hunters wore. This garment consisted of hundreds of a kind of fir cone stitched on to fabric. In addition, many of the children wore light helmets adorned with fur and upstanding ears. It was hard to tell them from the true dogs. Their hands, their knees, their feet, were calloused and pad-like. Many of them had sharp faces, as if in imitation of canine muzzles.

While the dog-pack cavorted and peered into the faces of their captives, the hunters were busy ransacking everything piled on the luggage trolley. The tourists had an unrivaled view of knees and scarred calves, and could listen to the harsh language of their captors. More hunters and dogs emerged from nowhere and ringed them round. Rain began to fall in ponderous drops.

Dulcifer pulled himself into a sitting position, arms folded over knees.

"They haven't killed us outright. What do you suppose they will do with us?"

"Depends on whether or not I've killed their chief," Takeido said. "They're looking into that now." He began laughing miserably until Constanza hushed him.

The rain fell more heavily. The chief had been carried off the road. They knew his position by the knot of hunters surrounding him. The sky was dark.

"Why don't those damned buses return for us?" Constanza asked. "I know those foolish hostesses, Sonya Rykznel, Bonni Fin, Pru Ganin. Why have they not become alarmed and turned back to look for us?"

Rain poured down their faces. They were already soaked to the skin. Water hissed and bubbled off the smooth surface of the road. They waited. Kordan hid his face in his hands.

"I am a mere Academician, not a leader . . . There is a great difference . . ."

"I have been thinking about what was said earlier," Burek spoke at last. "They regard us as protein. They will exploit us as food. They have no human values. After all, once a capitalist enemy, always a capitalist enemy. We are in a bad position—I remember an old saying, 'A man in a lion's den turns to wolves for friendship.' "

"If we return to the System, I shall put in a severe criticism," said Sygiek. "All these creatures should have been destroyed before the planet was opened to tourism. The Minister for Outourism must answer for this. The propaganda also was misleading. I would not have come here had I known the true state of affairs."

"Agreed," said Kordan. "Outourist is notoriously lax. All the same, my orders were disobeyed. Utopianist Takeido, you will be criticized for firing your flare-gun without permission."

The rain plastered their hair against their foreheads. The dogs whined and slunk ceaselessly about them.

Takeido brushed moisture from his face and glared across at Kordan. "Academician Kordan, I tell you now, just in case they set the hounds on us in a minute or two and we are torn to bits, I don't give a cuss for you or your stupid authority. When we met in the hotel, I thought you were a great and wise man—now I have a contempt for you. We are fifty light years from the System, so forget about it, forget the System! It's only a prison, with your kind as jailers. Right, Vul Dulcifer?"

Dulcifer shrugged his shoulders. "But you are so like them, Ian Takeido—always appealing to someone else for support. In the world in which we are forced to live, each individual has to guard his own heart."

"What do you say, Mystery Man, Che Burek?" asked Takeido, wiping rain impatiently from his lips. "Have you a similarly feeble answer to Utopianist Dulcifer's? Or a rustic saying of no marked relevance? Or are you a secret member of the USRP?"

Constanza's hand went to her lips. "Don't speak like that, Ian!"

"I say that we are not dead yet, and that there may still be hope if we cease quarreling with each other. Remember the old saying, 'When the frogs croak loudest, the crane strikes.' " Burek illustrated with a hard hand, jabbing sharply toward the freeway. "You are young, Ian Takeido—you don't understand that rain isn't the only way of getting wet."

"You men are fools," Sygiek said, glaring with contempt over the spiked backs of hounds. "You in particular, Takeido. Do you imagine for one moment that because you are out of the System that the system is out of you? We are its products, stamped with it through and through, as much shaped by it as these degenerate barbarians are by their environment."

"I couldn't have uttered a harsher criticism of you myself," said Takeido.

Still the rain dropped down, filling the air with liquid sound. The landscape appeared to dissolve in water. Hunters, dogs, and children kept up their ceaseless activity, milling over the area, always maintaining watch in all directions. At length, the hunter chief was helped to his feet. He shook his spear above his skull-crowned head. A cheer went up, the dogs barked and whined.

At the same time, as if the two events were connected, the downpour tapered off sharply. One of the zebras was kicked to its feet and the chief mounted unaided. Again a cheer arose. He pointed toward the six prisoners.

More activity, more yapping from dogs and children. The tourists were made to rise to their feet. They stood dripping and dashing the last of the rain from their eyes. Willing hands pulled them down from the road, splashing through muddy water toward the spot where the chief waited.

A long pole was brought. Hempen ropes appeared. The six were lashed to the pole in a row, with hands secured behind their backs so that they could only proceed forward in line abreast. To add to their humiliation, packs of provisions and some of the looted articles from the luggage trolley were strapped to their shoulders so that they became beasts of burden as well as prisoners.

While this was happening, hunters and hounds alike were disappearing into the waterlogged countryside, into gulleys and scrub. Before they knew it, the forlorn knot of utopians was again alone with its original five assailants.

VII

A harsh order was given. The six captives were made to march forward, yoked like oxen, into the semi-desert. Yellow mud splashed about their ankles with every step. Their heads were down and they moved for a long while in silence.

"The rain will never fertilize this ground," said Takeido. "I would love to do some soil-analysis—you would expect to find an almost total absence of micro-organisms. No doubt that was why the crops failed when the colonists first crash-landed here. Vital links in the chain of life have yet to form. What a rotten planet to pick to land on."

"With a minimum of terraforming, this could be a good planet," replied Dulcifer. Nobody else said anything. With their heads bent and the difficulties underfoot, they felt disinclined for conversation.

"We'll turn this into an endless carpet of wheat in a century," Dulcifer said. Nobody answered him.

Time passed. The tourists lost account of it, in their increasing weariness. Their minds grew blank as every step became an effort. They gazed down at their muddied feet in dull animal pain.

Abruptly, their captors made them change direction and halt behind a pile of boulders crowned by ferns. The hunters dismounted, whereupon their steeds fell to the soggy ground as if dead. One hunter stood guard while the other four vanished rapidly among nearby boulders.

Minutes later, a terrible squealing sounded, followed

by a deep silence. When the hunters reappeared, each held the leg of an ungainly creature swinging at arm's length between them. Laughing in triumph, they threw the carcass down by their captives.

In this creature, adaptation from the standard human form had been carried to an amazing degree.

It was truly four-legged. In death, the larger hind legs doubled under its lean belly. It otherwise resembled a boar. What had been separate digits in the front legs of its ancestors had through usage become welded into horny hooves.

Eyes unwinking in death, it glared up at the downcast faces of the humans. Two small tusks, adaptations of canine teeth, curled outward from the upper jaw, raising the lip in a sneer. It was covered in short bristles and even boasted a short tail. Yet the horror lay not in its resemblance to an animal but in its resemblance to a man.

With business-like speed, the hunters hammered a spiked pole through the boar's body from anus to mouth and balanced it on their shoulders. Using kicks and curses, they drove the panting zebras to their feet. Then they kicked the prisoners from their lethargy. The procession got under way again. The ground dried underfoot.

As the hours passed, the enforced march began to go harder with the prisoners. Their feet hurt, every muscle in their legs aching, the chafing of the pole on their shoulders became intolerable. They moaned for water and rest.

The day was well eroded before they were allowed another halt. For the last two hours, they had been moving steadily uphill, winding a painful way over gravelly slopes. As soon as they were permitted to stop, they fell to the ground in the same manner as the zebras.

Liquid noises caught their attention.

They came to observe that they were lying by a pool of water set amid rock. A stream ran invitingly into the pool. Pebbles gleamed under the surface, little fish fled or meditated on impossible missions. Freshwater shrimps toyed with freedom only a few centimeters from their eyes.

The hunters drank first, then their zebra-mounts. Finally the prisoners were allowed to drink and dunk their burning heads and shoulders in the cool liquid. While they lay there groaning, one of the hunters came with a flint knife and cut their bonds, so that they were free of the pole. Frugally, he gathered up the rope, stowing it away while they massaged their limbs.

Sygiek looked about. Behind them, to the west, a sullen glory was gathering in the low clouds. The planet lay beneath the clouds, rumpled and meaningless. Of course there was no sight of the road. And the silence was the silence of a continent unready for life.

Constanza crawled to Sygiek's side. "I'm sure that the other buses have returned and rescued the rest of our party by now. Do you think they'll be able to track us across this wilderness?"

"They don't have to follow on land. There are flycraft and matboats in Peace City that will search us out."

"Of course, but nobody would ever see us from the air in this sort of country. Besides, it will be getting dark soon."

"Infra-red will soon detect us, by day or night."

"Utopianist Sygiek, the question is whether they will be in time, isn't it? These primitive beings have very different attitudes to females from true men. Atavistic, repulsive. I heard a few disgusting tales from women who worked on building the road and I don't mind telling you I'm scared about our possible fate. You know what I mean —some nauseating mass sexual experience."

Sygiek laughed and patted her arm. "Don't worry about that. We certainly don't look very attractive at the moment, do we?"

Constanza glanced down at her breasts, and pulled her stained uniform together. "It's not so much the look as the shape, I believe."

Easing his way to Dulcifer, Kordan said, "You see that line of hills ahead? They must be taking us there, presuming they need to be home by nightfall. Can you make out caves in the cliff-face? These savages are probably troglodytes. This might be our last chance to escape. Do you feel like making a break for it and running back to the bus?"

"No."

"No, nor do I. I can hardly move another pace."

Flat on his stomach, Dulcifer looked cautiously about. The hunters were sitting relaxedly nearby, talking among themselves. Kordan lay next to him; the others were also grouped about the pool: Burek, Takeido, then the two women. Catching Burek's eye, he reached down into the pool and took a fair-sized stone in his fist. He motioned to the others to do the same. With the exception of Kordan, they all chose a stone.

They lay as if dead, letting the water ripple over their flesh.

The hunters had come to a decision. Two of them set their spears down and walked briskly over to their captives. They gave a hoarse command. When there was no response, they kicked out at exposed flanks.

As Dulcifer felt the sandal on his calf, he turned, grasped the hunter's leg, and flung him down to the ground. While his opponent was falling, he brought up his right arm and struck with the stone. Dulcifer had overestimated his reserves of strength—he missed the hunter's skull and caught him on the chin. The hunter fell heavily but instantly counter-attacked and had Dulcifer by the throat before he could strike a second time. The stone was wrenched from his grasp and flung away.

The other tourists fared no better. Constanza and Sygiek dragged a second hunter down between them but did not manage to still his furious struggles. He called for help. The other hunters came over at a run. Burek met them bravely, with Takeido giving rather hesitant support, but in no time they were flat on the ground. Takeido nursed a bleeding lip. The struggle was over.

"You have some rotten ideas, Comrade Dulcifer," Takeido said. "I'm disillusioned with you, too, if you wish to know."

"You fools!" cried Kordan. "You will get us all killed. Why don't you obey orders?"

A hunter kicked him savagely in the back, and he sprawled with his companions. He lay there miserably while Sygiek stroked his shoulder.

They were secured again. Their wrists were tied painfully behind their necks. This time, the pole was dispensed with.

"Well, at least we tried . . . It's obvious their intention is not to slit our guts out," said Dulcifer.

"Wolves prefer their food fresh," replied Burek, grimly.

As they prepared to move forward, more natives materialized from the rocks.

The newcomers were not of the hunter caste. Their faces were unpainted. They wore no barbed coats; their one garment was a kind of loin-cloth, concealing their genitals. About their heads, their hair fanned out in extraordinary fashion, so as to resemble a kind of helmet. In their leather belts were small clubs or hammers. They crowded round the captives in curiosity, prodding and laughing, but the hunters made them keep their distance. They were given the spitted boar to carry.

"Culturally speaking, this is a valuable experience," said Kordan.

The ground crumbled underfoot as they climbed toward the cliffs. There was no grass to bind the soil. Every step was a labor. The captives were panting heavily before they were stopped again. They had arrived at the cliffs. They had arrived at a settlement.

Between the newcomers and the cliffs ran a swift river, spanned by a rough wooden bridge. At cave-mouths in the cliff, warriors sat relaxedly on watch. These warriors called a greeting to the hunters, the chief of whom gave a triumphant cry in return.

The bridge was guarded by sentries, and by an elaborately carved pole, with bogey-man faces set one above the other, grimacing hideously at new arrivals. The sentries wore similar masks, carved from wood. They waited without impatience.

As they rested, Takeido said to Constanza. "It is hard to realize this is actually happening. It shows up a bad flaw in the System."

"What will become of us?" sighed Constanza. "These people are utterly inhuman. Wearing masks . . . it's absurd and revolting."

"If we knew the truth," replied Burek, "we would probably admire the heroism of this group of savages. They are the descendants of the original colonists who have managed to stay human, or more or less human, while all the others have gradually deteriorated into beasts. That's 1.09 million E-years of bitterest struggle for survival! I am in part glad to be here, for to me the tale of Lysenka II, if it can ever be fully told, is a fable of triumph as well as horror."

For him it was a long speech, but Sygiek would have nothing of it.

"On the contrary, it is a tale of degradation," she said. "Think how much progress we have made on Earth in the equivalent time, not least in surviving nine ice ages and rationalizing the irrational."

Dulcifer touched her arm. "It would be rational to accept both Burek's view and your own. Let's keep an open mind and we may yet escape—you're a strong character and you can do that. I admire the way you speak out, but I counsel tact."

She gave him a shy smile.

Despite his weariness, Kordan turned to Dulcifer, saying sharply, "The way in which you assume a relationship between Millia Sygiek and yourself is incorrect. We are well aware that you come from Iridium City, but the closeness you adopt is improper. Please restrain yourself."

Dulcifer said, "I'm sorry it upsets you. Relationships don't come at our beck and call. Even Biocom hasn't made us that rational."

Sygiek hung her head, aware that his words had unexpectedly brought tears to her eyes. She looked surreptitiously round at her companions, filthy and abject, at the alien hunters, painted to look alarming, at the wooden masks of the sentries, at the whole meager tan scene.

Ignoring Kordan, she said to Dulcifer, "A sudden recollection . . . Why should I remember that? Of course I was an exobirth, brought up for my first ten years in the crèche of the country town of Akrakt. I was always in trouble. I had no friends among all the hundreds of my siblings. The machines used to down-rate me and I was punished. I spent many hours alone in the dormitory during the day, just looking out of the window. Outside was an old peach orchard. I don't know why I tell you this."

"Well, let's find out," said Dulcifer. "Go on."

"There was some local planning dispute, I believe. So the old peach orchard remained at the back of the crèche. I thought the neglected trees very beautiful . . . There were two women who worked in the crèche, prole women. They were large and shapeless. One, I remember, had black hair which was tied to hang down her back like a horse's tail. They liked to walk in the derelict orchard. I must once have known their names. I used to envy the women. They walked so close, heads together, talking, half-smiling. How I used to wonder if they were sisters, and what they talked about . . .

"And they would stand under the trees and lift their fat bare arms and pluck the golden fruit. They used to gather it in their arms and eat with the juice running down their chins, laughing. Not pleasant, really—but to me then, as a lonely child, so pleasant, so very pleasant. They were so happy and in such communion. Do you see what I mean?"

"You should have called to them," Dulcifer said. "They would have liked your company. They would have given you peaches."

"I never had the courage to call to them. I kept my window closed."

"It's hard to ask for what we want most, isn't it?" He regarded her almost shyly.

She kicked the ground at her feet and did not reply.

They had halted at the bridge to allow the chief hunter to transfer his captives officially to the sentries. First went the spitted boar.

The transaction took place as a slow ceremony. The commander of the sentries, a sturdy man with bow legs and a head thrust forward from rounded shoulders, gave a salute of thanks. The chief returned it, touching the skull on his head. Then the prisoners were prodded across the bridge. The hunters stayed on their own side, stiff and watchful.

As they crossed the bridge, Takeido looked back and gave the chief a mocking salute of farewell. The chief did not respond.

So they arrived under the towering cliff, its face pocked with entrances. From one hole, a stream gushed, falling free to splash among rocks and feed the river. To other holes, ladders led. There was very little activity, the sentries at the cave-mouths always expected. In the graying light, the place presented a dismal appearance; to the utopians, accustomed to their graceful pyramidal cities, it looked like a rats' warren, awaiting extermination.

The prisoners' bonds were cut. They were driven by the sentries to climb one of the ladders. It was about seven meters high, and groaned and swayed as they climbed. A guard at the top hauled them one by one into the mouth of the cave.

VIII

They were made to squat at the entrance of the cave, as if in preparation for a long wait.

They had the outside world to sit and look back on as they rested. An uncomforting place it was: the ruinous landscape was now loaded with grey; it was that time of evening when the brightness in the sky merely accentuated the darkness gathered on the ground. The hunters who had captured them were allowed over the bridge. As they trundled across, round-shouldered and no longer alert, the chief removed the skull from his head to swing it at arm's length with a thumb hooked in one eye-socket.

A pack of mongrels was unleashed to patrol the cliff-foot; the melancholy howling of the creatures reinforced a general desolation.

Yet, forbidding as it was, all this formed part of a world the captives knew. As such, it appeared desirable in comparison with the dark warrens into which the tunnel behind them led. Noises and odors were wafted to them from that direction on a clammy wind; none was appealing.

"You don't need reminding that we are in deep trouble," said Kordan, speaking in a low voice. "Without consulting me, you attacked the guards and were inevitably defeated. Such undisciplined behavior has lessened our chance of reaching any form of agreement with these savages. What you hoped could be gained by it, I can't imagine."

It was the youngest member of the party, Ian Takeido,

who answered him. "Without disrespect, Utopianist Kordan, that is exactly your problem—being unable to imagine. Imagination is necessary for control of the outside world." He closed his eyes tightly as he spoke. "When any new thing is presented to our senses, it is only with the aid of imagination that we can appreciate to which value-group it belongs and rank it accordingly. Reason alone is not sufficient. I daresay you would agree with me there, Che Burek?"

"To put it bluntly, no," said Burek. "I think you are a bit of an intellectual prig, comrade, and I can't see that imagination will get us home."

"He's not a prig!" exclaimed Constanza, putting an arm defensively round Takeido. "Even if he does say some indiscreet things."

"Perhaps, Utopianist Takeido, you will be good enough to imagine us back to the safety of Unity," Kordan said, smiling thinly as if in pain.

"Imagination is not a trick but a principle of life," Takeido answered, biting at his knuckles. "What we should determine, whilst there is time, is to what category these creatures belong."

"That's intellectual rubbish," said Burek. "Remember the old saying, 'It doesn't matter if the honey does not forgive the bear.' The point is that *they* decide in which category *we* belong—protein category, most likely." He leaned back contentedly against a rock, folding his arms.

"That sort of defeatist answer proves my point," said Takeido, his eyebrows moving rapidly up and down with nervousness. "Our image of these savages has been *ad hoc* all along. First as animals, then as capitalists, now as cannibals. I'm sorry you choose to disagree with me and insult me, Utopianist Burek, because in fact I take my cue from something you said when we were waiting at the bridge, about the story of Lysenka II being, not a story of defeat, but a fable of triumph. If only our imagination will permit us to encompass a few millennia, we may perceive that these beings are in a super-category above animal, capitalist, cannibal, a super-category not unlike our own. They also are trapped on an alien planet—a planet that can never cease to remain alien however long they or their descendants exist here. So we can find common cause with them.

We *all* need to get off Lysenka II. With that cause established—and communication must be possible—we become
allies rather than enemies and can negotiate with them. In
exchange for our freedom, the system agrees to settle
Lysenka's human tribes on Earth."

Sygiek clapped her hands. "Brilliant deductions. I said
reason was needed."

"Brilliant imagination," said Kordan. "And nothing more.
We have been accustomed all our life to what you call
negotiation; it is our directing principle. Do you think
these barbarians, on their uncompromising world, will
understand such a concept? I doubt it! For them, it must
inevitably be a quick meal today rather than rescue next
year."

"You will accept nothing you do not think of yourself,"
said Constanza angrily.

Dulcifer and Sygiek remained outside the discussion
which then took place. He put his arm round her blistered
shoulder and she leaned against his comforting bulk. After
a while, he said in her ear, "When we attacked the hunters
at the pool, why did you not use your gun? You could
have killed all five of them. I'm sure killing is not against
your principles as it is Kordan's."

"Yes, I would have used the gun," she said, so quietly
that he alone could hear. "Only I do not possess it any
more. I must have lost it—or somebody stole it from me."

They sat and looked at each other. He dropped his
gaze first, sighing wearily. Then he looked up again,
grinned, and said, "Peach trees!"

From the gloom of the tunnel, three savages emerged.
One collected the boar from the custody of the guards,
shouldered it, and disappeared again, bent double. The
other two carried staves with which they prodded the
prisoners to their feet. They bowed with an uncouth courtesy before searching them. This search was carried out
perfunctorily.

"We wish to go before your praesidium," said Kordan.
"We have no intention of harming you. Do you understand?"

The guards took no notice. They saluted the sentries at
the tunnel-mouth and motioned with their staves for the
tourists to walk before them into the darkness. Constanza

clung to Takeido as they went, for it was wet underfoot. Cold drops of water came winging down from the roof and splashed on their heads. Shelves of fungi grew on outcrops of rock to one side. They staggered along unsurely.

"Oh, powers, this is all a nightmare!" groaned Kordan. "How I long for the safety of the Academy again!"

Somewhere ahead, a light burned. At closer quarters it proved to be a rough lamp, either of stone or pottery, marking a sharp bend in the tunnel with its uneasy flame. Past the bend stood a wooden stockade. The gate in the middle of the stockade was closed from the inside. Sentries in helmets looked curiously down at the prisoners from a platform set behind the barrier. No move was made to open the gate.

"Now what are we waiting for?" Sygiek demanded of the escort. She received no answer. The escort stood impassively, letting water drip over their skulls and down their cheeks.

Sygiek shivered. She was tired and cold. On the gate of the stockade was emblazoned one of the bogey-man faces. She turned away from it in loathing and said to Kordan, "Why don't they answer me? They have a language."

He laid a hand affectionately on her arm. "They will have their instructions. They may attach some significance to waiting before entrances which means nothing to us. If they have been told not to speak, they do not speak. For all our respect for language, you and I would do the same. Looking at these creatures, I can't help thinking about this whole amazing paradox of the recession of the Lysenkan colonists into kinds of animals. I believe that language is the key to the mystery."

"Why do you say 'amazing paradox'? Without suitable structural social context, people decline. That's a truism."

Standing huddled together in the semi-darkness as they were, they found any conversation tended to become general. Constanza agreed with Sygiek. "Quite so. The organization withers, the individual is left. Then anarchy follows. The Lysenkan menagerie forms a perfect illustration of the truth of system doctrine."

Kordan shook his head. "Without wishing to argue against doctrine, I must point out that it was inevitably by breaking new ground, by forming new tribes, new tongues, new societies, that *homo sapiens* developed in the first place. Let me explain that such a reversion from manhood to animalhood as we witness on Lysenka runs contrary to evolutionary law as explicated by K. V. Hondaras over two thousand years ago. That is why I speak of a paradox." He paused and then said hesitantly, "Accepting official explanations, I could scarcely believe that the colonists could have degenerated into those various forms we saw with our own eyes."

They fell silent, listening to the water drip into the mud underfoot, until Constanza said, "Did you believe that what you saw was some kind of propaganda-trick?"

Takeido said, "Excuse me, but the means of evolution are well understood. Duplicate genes provide spare copies in which changes can be accumulated. For an alien strain on Lysenka, changes would be rapid, and the human stock would respond rapidly to natural selection. Where's your difficulty?"

"Ah, but what of social selection? These people we're talking about may have been capitalists but they had comparatively high social organizations. For pre-utopian days." Kordan hesitated, then plunged in as if deciding that he must talk. "We have spoken all along of these unfortunates in terms of *function*, as protein-eaters, or capitalists, or colonists. But when their starship crash-landed here, they were bereft of function in that sense. They became passive, malleable, in an evolutionary sense. Reduced to bare existence, they would have been forced by the sterility of Lysenka II to spread out thinly in order to survive on what food there was, digging roots, picking berries, searching for insects under stones . . . They would be Gatherers, not Hunters, at first. I can imagine that it would take only one generation for them to revert to complete primitivism. Those who could not or would not revert would die off."

Burek grunted, ". . . Or hold the ship and its supplies against all comers and survive that way . . ."

"A wasting asset," said Dulcifer.

" 'As the teat grows thinner, the kid sucks with greater vehemence,' " Burek replied.

The sentries had disappeared from the top of the stockade, but still there was no move to open the gate. The prisoners leaned against the damp rock walls, and Kordan said, "Let me make my point, please. Degeneration is not the same as mutation. How did these people become animal? By renouncing their humanity: an involuntary process. And how was that done? Because they lost the one basic art which makes us *homo uniformis* and which made them human, the art of language. From his animal forebears, *homo sapiens* inherited the frozen vocabulary of instinct, and developed it over the millennia into a complex mode of expression whereby he could control, firstly, himself, and then the world. Expression. What does language express? Language is transitive. Between total language and the nature of the cosmos lies a close relationship; indeed, according to Hondaras, mind is the high-point of cosmos, and man' the expression of its emergent characteristic. Mind's vehicle is language. In the End will be only the Word."

Sygiek said, "Despite the orthodoxy of K. V. Hondaras's work, this speculation is still contentious."

"We rightly label all speculation contentious," Kordan replied. "Yet here and now we are forced into a speculative posture. What is sure is that the stranded colonists were faced with disorientation, complete mental disorientation. Time was wrong; the earth failed them. They would have run up against an immutable law which all societies prefer to forget as they become sophisticated: that there is not only no civilization but practically no basis for life where there are no crops. Those tragic colonists planted their grain. It rotted in the ground. Fertilizers had no effect. The land, the time, was against them."

He stared up at the distant roof of rock. It was barely visible in the gloom. Only one or two stalactites showed, like distorted stars.

"No doubt they turned to magic when science failed. Magic and incantation take us back to the roots of language and the power of repetition. But magic also failed. The cosmos was shown to be defective."

He pursed his lips. "Try to imagine what they were up against. Human experience proved insufficient to counter their new inhuman experience. They were driven back to instinctual behavior—the subsistence-level of thinking of the Gatherer—and instinct is ultimately the enemy of language.

78

That one unique feature, the pact between the codes of language and the cosmos, was broken for the first time in the history of mankind. In the resulting anomic situation, genetic equilibrium would be disrupted, and the way laid open for regression to animal modes. We are fortunate in that at least we have fallen into the hands of a group which has managed to retain some humanity. It may be such a group as Burek postulates, which managed to hold the original ship and so retain more firmly than other groups old values, including language."

Takeido was shivering with cold. Clutching his upper arms, he said, "Don't be so optimistic. I take a gloomy view of the symbolism of this dark tunnel they have led us into."

Dulcifer had been leaning against the tunnel wall, scarcely bothering to listen to the talk. Now he seized on a point that Kordan had made earlier. Wiping the moisture from his face, he looked closely at the other and asked, "Which are you going to believe, then, Kordan? The official line as laid down by K. V. Hondaras, or the evidence of your own eyes?"

"It is a test, isn't it? Perhaps that's why this planet is closed to all but the privileged—it's a world which doesn't fit into our system. Perhaps that's why it's *open* to the privileged—they can be tested . . ."

Then Kordan looked around and said no more, gnawing anxiously at his lower lip.

"Aren't you going to give me an answer, you who are so fond of answers?" said Dulcifer, mockingly. "Put it into language for us. 'Never think what cannot be said.' "

"Are you a provocateur or something? Leave him alone," Burek said, giving Dulcifer a shove. "Maybe Kordan prefers not to say what cannot be thought. What he tells us is interesting, as far as I understood it, and I don't see why philosophy should cover all contingencies of reality, else philosophy and reality would be indistinguishable—and plainly that was never intended."

"Who's to say what's intended any more?" Takeido muttered. They stood there in the mud, occasionally lifting a foot. At last the bolts on the stockade gate were withdrawn, and the escort stepped smartly forward to drive its party through. Once they were in, the gate was closed behind them.

Mud still lay thick underfoot, though there was an encouraging light ahead. Planking and logs had been laid in the mud. From this main tunnel, side tunnels branched. As they went ahead again, picking their way, the darkness became less intense. At last, the tunnel opened into a large chamber, which was well lighted. To one side of this chamber, a cage built of wood had been set up. The guards forced their prisoners into the cage and secured it shut.

IX

Trapped under the epidermis of an alien planet, surrounded by a savage species the more terrible for resembling men, threatened by all manner of fates, the six weary
utopians enjoyed the luxury of Biocom: they controlled
their thoughts and allowed their unified nervous systems
to calm them. There was room in the cage for them all to
sit, and it was dry. So they sat down, rested, and awaited
events.

When their eyes grew accustomed to the gloom, they
gained a better impression of the cavern to which they had
been brought. It was lit by a few flambeaux standing out
from the rock at intervals, and by a fire which burned on a
stone in the middle of the enormous space. There were
two other, much dimmer, sources of light.

Firstly, on the far side of the cavern, a hole overhead
gave a glimpse of the sky. In the general confusion of
shadows and structures which filled the area, this hole
was not immediately apparent. Once they perceived it, the
prisoners realized with dismay that the outside world was
almost as dark as the world inside, and that Lysenka II
was already turning toward its lengthy night period.

Secondly, also on the far side of the cavern, a large
building stood. Upon the steps of this building, a number
of candles burned, casting the shadows of its columns into
the interior. The building was circular in ground plan, and
roofless. Its elegance set it at variance with the general

roughness of its surroundings. Between its colonnades, a shadowy metal mass could be observed, as well as a ladder-like structure pointing to the hole in the roof above. Puzzle as they might, the prisoners could not make out the function of this building, although as time passed, a number of savages took up candles from the steps, went inside, and paraded formally round.

When the small patch of sky was entirely dark, many more people entered the cavern. They came in quietly, and paraded in little groups. All were roughly clad. There were babies and small children among them, none of whom uttered a sound. The cave-dwellers flocked in from various entrances. Opposite the cage was a tunnel mouth, down which the flow of torches could be seen for some while before their bearers reached the central chamber.

The company made a slow promenade of the cavern, each group halting when it got to the cage to look in at its inhabitants. Instinctively, the utopians rose to their feet and stared back. The cave-dwellers appeared reserved, even respectful, but their dark faces were expressionless. Then they moved on, and went through complicated charades, almost as if performing a dumb-show; the meaning of this performance was lost on the watchers.

Following the dumb-show came a massed entrance into the far building. The cave-dwellers could be seen among the pillars, rubbing the complex metal structures with their hands. There were strange cries. Gongs and trumpets sounded.

After this ceremony, the atmosphere became more relaxed. Family groups assembled round the central fire. An aged woman in a flowing gown emerged from the shadows and related, with plentiful gestures, what sounded like a long dull story.

"The father and the mother perform sexual intercourse, after which the child is born from inside the mother's body," said Burek, looking up from a reverie. "I saw a reconstruction of the event in a visionshow, and it must have been extremely painful, except that, as the saying has it, 'The cow expects nothing but what happens to cows.' You see these primitives also keep their children with them because they have no experts to teach them to grow adult properly, as with us. The whole science of adoleschematics has not been invented as far as these wretches are concerned."

"Some of them are eating now," said Constanza. "At least we are not on their menu tonight. Rescue must arrive by morning. Why are the squads taking so long?"

From a side-tunnel, platters of steaming food were emerging, carried by women in aprons. They were accompanied by a man with a big bag slung about his belly. He took tokens of some kind from everyone who accepted food. The watchers could not understand the meaning of this.

Takeido sniffed. "Cooking smells good. Do we get any?"

"Inevitably, they are eating animal or else their fellows," said Kordan. "Such a diet would make us ill."

"I would try it," said Takeido. "Terror makes you hungry. I must eat or sit and scream."

"I have eaten animal and come to no harm," said Dulcifer. *Sotto voce*, he added in Sygiek's ear. "And I fancy you had to do so as part of your USRP training."

She silenced him by putting her fingers over his mouth.

When the food scraps were being cleared away, the comparative quiet of the cavern was broken by the entry of capering animals.

Two of them rushed in, followed by cave-dwellers with whips, which they cracked vigorously. These animals were immediately recognized as carnivores. The shape of their skulls was predetermined, not by cortical development, but by the large lower jaw, to which the rest of the head appeared subordinate. Fearsome fangs were in evidence, as the creatures snarled at their tormentors. Their bodies were lean, most of the musculature and weight going into shoulders, forelegs and hindlegs. For all their animality, and their spotted hide, the basic human form was apparent —most apparent when they pranced on their hindlegs. Garments had been tied round their necks and on their heads by their tormentors, increasing the effect of cruel parody.

The leopard-like animals were driven round in a circle by their tormentors. The onlookers, sitting cross-legged with their children, clapped their hands and chanted monotonously. The chant rose to a crescendo. Gongs sounded again. With strange automatic gestures the tormentors dropped their whips, drew long swords and rushed in on the animals. Crying piteously, the leopards tried to escape. Their hindlegs had been shackled. After one or two thrusts they collapsed, writhing, and their bodies were seized and lifted high. Blood flowed. More chanting.

Everyone rose. The killers led a procession round the whole cavern area and then into the pillared building. They fell silent.

A tall man dressed in what aspired to be a uniform, with gloves, long boots, and a transparent helmet over his head, appeared from the darkness at the rear of the temple. He stood silent while the dead beasts were laid upon the stone before him. He dipped his hands in their blood. Then he strode over to the shadowy blocks of metal, where several attendants, also dressed in vestigial uniforms, waited. All began to rub and prod the arrangements of rods and casings. The audience took up a low chant.

The tall man walked to a chair placed beside the metal arrangement. Deep drums throbbed. Their beat grew more deafening. The tall man pulled a lever. Faster beat the drums. The seat tipped back, turning into a couch. The drums thundered, the audience screamed at the top of its lungs. Back went the couch, up went the arm of the rider. The noise died to a whisper, the ghost of a whisper. The finger on the end of the arm pointed up, up into the murk, to the patch of open sky. The clouds had rolled away.

In that patch of sky, one star burned.

The ceremony was suddenly over. The magic was done. The tall man climbed from his couch. Children started crying and running amid the throng, as everyone began to go home.

"I never thought to see . . ." Kordan said. "Ritual . . . it was a primitive *ritual*—forms of conduct fixed and repeated, the satisfaction of pattern reinforcing lifestyle."

"You could be right," said Dulcifer. "I've watched Venusian desert-skimmers performing the same meaningless acts over and over. Presumably they reinforce the image of themselves as desert-skimmers that way."

"Why should they put on such a performance for us?" asked Sygiek.

"There you show your lack of that imagination I spoke of before we came in here," said Takeido excitedly. "They are doing it for themselves—we don't come into it. Not yet. I believe Kordan to be substantially correct. I had forgotten the word even: *ritual*. Performing the same acts over and over, reinforcing an image. Man's distant ape ancestors on Earth may have had to perform such meaningless acts over many generations before they became human."

"But these are not meaningless acts, Ian Takeido," said Kordan. "For us, certainly not for them. Now I ask *you* to exercise your imagination. Imagine that capitalist ship over one million years ago. Imagine its survivors forced into various ecological niches in order to survive, losing language and human identity. How many creatures have spread and multiplied across Lysenka, surviving the impoverished Devonian? Several million? I don't know. But we have the evidence of our eyes that one of those unfortunate groups—and it may be small, may consist of no more than a couple of hundred individuals—has managed to maintain its humanity more or less intact, using hierarchy and ritual to reinforce its distinctness from the creatures on which it must prey."

"You speak almost with compassion, Jerezy Kordan," said Burek.

"It's no good being sympathetic to these monsters, Utopianist Kordan," said Constanza. "They certainly aren't sympathetic to us. If they don't rape or kill us tonight, they will in the morning. They are animals. They have not fed us. They have not given us water. Soon we're going to *have to use this cage as a latrine, which is disgusting.

"Even if what you say is true—and personally I don't give a fig what happened in the past—you are only talking about an extension of the illegal capitalist system, aren't you? Surely our basic utopian beliefs are put to the test right here. If all the rest of the colonists went under and just this human group survived to prey on the rest, then these are the exploiter class, the bourgeois rabble of Lysenka, and there is more reason to eliminate them than all the rest. Here is the ideological enemy. When we are rescued, they will all be shot."

Silence fell.

"An unexpected speech from you, Comrade Constanza," said Burek, in his deep, rather mocking voice.

"Oh, I know you think I'm just a fool. I think that you

are one more élitist bore, Utopianist Burek, and I'm vexed
that I am now forced to make water in your presence. Turn
your backs, all of you."

The cavern had emptied except for two forlorn bent figures, extinguishing candles on the far steps. The crowd had
disappeared into side-tunnels, stumbling off to sleep out
the long Lysenkan night. The six prisoners sat in their
cage.

In a minute, Kordan began speaking again. His voice
trembled at first. "I know I am a poor leader. Equally, you
are poor followers. Our situation is unparalleled. I see
that Rubyna Constanza is ideologically correct. I also
see that Ian Takeido is right. We have to think in more
than one context, and that is always uncomfortable; inevitably, such is often my duty as historian.

"By the way, I must apologize if my earlier remarks
about language-failure causing evolutionary breakdown
sounded unorthodox. I did speak unguardedly. I was thinking out what I would say when I got back to the Academy . . .

"We must sometimes look beyond our necessary vigilance against enemies of the system. What we have witnessed here, I believe, is a ritual which dates back to that
seminal event in the generations of these debased creatures:
an attempt to get their damaged ship off this planet and
back into space. Over the ages, that ambition lost its force;
urgency has become ceremony; the meaning is now in the
means; but the means reinforces their besieged sense of
identity. Though the idea of space travel has dwindled to
no more than a religion, that religion helps them remain
human."

"Remain capitalist, you mean," said Constanza, with
contempt.

"*Religion!*" exclaimed Takeido. "That's the word I was
after. Jaini Regentop mentioned religion. It means a kind
of faith. We have just witnessed a religious ceremony."
His eyebrows twitched again. "Religion was another of
those ancient enemies of the state. Before Biocom, the
internal workings of man's nervous systems were so confused—dating back as they did to his animal past—that he
was haunted by specters, one of which he dramatized as

86

an external supernatural being of great power who ordered things randomly, to man's advantage or disadvantage. These people have reverted to that state of superstition."

"Well, it's no concern of ours," said Burek, dismissing the subject, and yawning. "I shall follow our sagacious little Constanza's example, and then try to sleep. May I suggest we all do the same?"

"There may be a way of using these—hypotheses to our advantage," said Sygiek, ignoring him and addressing Kordan. "If these religious or ritualistic ideas you advance are near the truth, then the question to ask is, do these brutes know that we are from another world? If so, what will their attitude to us be?"

"A proper question, Millia," said Kordan. "I already had it in mind. Tomorrow, we may get a chance to impress them. There could be a way of working on their superstitious nature to our advantage. We are weary now; as Che Burek says, it is best that we should sleep if we can and face tomorrow with fresh hope."

"Agreed," said Dulcifer. "At least as far as the bit about sleep goes. Hope must look after itself."

They settled down uncomfortably within the confines of their prison.

Sygiek allowed Dulcifer to put his arms about her as she curled with her blistered shoulders against the bars of the cage. Close against his ear, she whispered, "I sense a change in Kordan. He is in command of himself again. I believe he stole my gun. There was a moment when he tried to caress me after the bureaucrat Morits died—that was when he took it from me."

Dulcifer nodded without commenting. "Sleep, my darling," he said. "Think of ancient peach trees and fat bare-armed women, and sleep."

The fires in the center of the cavern guttered in a clammy draft.

After the slow night, a slow day.

As soon as a faint grey light stole into the cavern, the cave-dwellers commenced various ritualistic attendances. Warriors came and went, blessed by minor dignitaries in the ceremonial building before proceeding further—presumably to hunt or patrol. Children were marshaled and taken through vigorous calisthentics. Women worked about the fires. The machine of the tribe was in action.

Food was brought early to the six captives. It came in a thick pottery bowl and consisted of a glutinous stew, with big chunks of meat lying in gravy. It steamed. There was also a large pitcher of water, which they passed round thankfully.

"We'd better eat," said Kordan. They stood staring down at the bowl which he held out to them.

"Looks good," said Dulcifer. He dipped a hand in, brought up some meat and thrust it into his mouth. The others watched him with fascination as he chewed.

"Eat," he said. "Eat. It's only our friend of yesterday, the boar."

One by one, they dipped in. Only Constanza refused.

"You are cannibals," she said. "It is against our ethics to taste this muck."

"You'll be hungry," Takeido warned. "Although it is nauseating, we need food. Never mind ideology, let me feed you, Rubyna!"

" 'Heroes never say no,' " Burek quoted.

"It's not too bad," said Sygiek, dipping in a second time. Constanza went and sat down at the far end of the cage. The others cleared the bowl between them.

They looked at each other with guilty smiles.

An aged crone brought another bowl. They cleared that too. Some water was left; after a brief debate, they washed their hands in it, and then emptied the pitcher on the floor. The crone brought a fresh pitcher, full of cold spring water. They said nothing. They drank till they gasped.

After the old woman had retrieved her pitcher, Sygiek went over to where Rubyna sat with Takeido.

"We must think positively," she said, looking down at the other woman. "Now that these savages have brought us underground, the chances of our being rescued by the forces from Peace City may be more remote than we estimated. So it is required of us that we keep up our strength. You made a mistake not eating."

"Go away," said Rubyna, sulkily. "Just because you ate that muck, you needn't force it down everyone's throat."

"We do what the system expects us to do. We must remain strong. Surely you understand that?"

Rubyna jumped up, facing the other woman, the pupils of her dark eyes wide. "Just don't give me orders, Millia Sygiek! You've done nothing but boss people around ever since you got in my bus, and I'm sick of the sound of your voice."

Sygiek stepped back, saying in a controlled tone, "Just behave yourself, you little Outourist girl. Some are qualified to give orders, some to take them."

"Well, you just make sure you know who is in which category before you open your mouth again! I haven't forgotten that you called me a worker. When we get out of here, you're going to have a very nasty surprise—you and those two fools who hang around sniffing your sloppy-maos!"

"Stop it, Constanza, stop it! We mustn't fight," cried Takeido, pulling her back. "We've got enough trouble without being divided amongst ourselves." He ran his hands over her red tunic, cupping her breasts. She turned and stared at him, as Kordan pulled Sygiek away and soothed her at the other end of the cage.

More time passed. A group of men, eight in number, came from an inner tunnel and marched purposefully to the cage. The captives stood and looked at them.

One of the cave-dwellers was the leader, the rest his retinue. There was no mistaking his authority. He was short, middle-aged, long-haired, dressed in a red cloak which hung from a wooden yoke at his shoulders. He wore a leather helmet. His manner was brisk, and he silenced a mutter which began among his attendants. He addressed his captives in a clattering burst of speech.

"We do not understand what you say," Kordan answered, "but before there can be any communication between us, we wish to leave this cage. Open the door."

He rattled the bars to demonstrate his meaning.

The leader said something, the others muttered behind him. Guards were called, moving up briskly with staves.

After a curt gesture from the leader, one of his henchmen stepped forward with a key and unlocked the cage door. He flung it wide. The captives came forth, Kordan first, then Burek, then Sygiek and Dulcifer, then Takeido, and Constanza last.

"We demand an escort to the safety of Dunderzee

Gorge," said Kordan. "We can offer you benefits in exchange. Do you understand?"

"They are hardly likely to understand, are they?" asked Sygiek.

"Very well, Millia—you put the message, over to them in sign language."

Sygiek turned to Constanza in conciliatory fashion. "You should know, Rubyna, you live on this beastly world —can anyone speak the language of these people?"

Rubyna turned a shoulder to the other man as she replied.

"They are not people but animals. We shoot them to kill them, like other animals. It is not even proved that they have a language; Kordan said as much. We shall be rescued soon, and then they will all be shot. Exterminated."

The leader put a hand on Kordan's arm. Kordan shrank back, but the gesture, though imperious, was not hostile. He was motioning them to follow him.

They had little choice. Despite the courtesy, they were carefully watched by guards, who hemmed them in as they walked across the rough floor, past the central fires, toward the religious building. At the steps of the building, the leader halted to harangue them again. His eye burned fiercely upon them, he spoke with fervor. He pointed frequently upward, one finger stretching to the hole in the cavern roof, through which clouded sky was visible. Then he addressed himself to Sygiek, speaking intensely to her, pointing at her and at himself.

She studied him intently, deliberately not dropping her gaze, trying to divine, through centuries of divergence, what kind of man he was. All she saw was the dark surface of his eyes. He produced from his tunic a shard of glass. It was part of a broken mirror. He held it up to her so that she saw her own grey eyes, then he pointed to his own face.

"What theories do you have about this?" she asked the others.

"He is asking you to mate with him," said Takeido, and sniggered.

"Maybe he had a daughter like you once," suggested Burek.

"He is commenting on facial similarities between our species and his," said Kordan.

90

"He is asking you to see that our kind and his are much alike," said Dulcifer, "and that you are much prettier than he is."

"He is going to cut your eyes out," said Constanza.

The question was not resolved. As if vexed, the leader made a signal with his left hand. The six were led up the steps and into the roofless building. As they passed, they saw men in robes making candles. They went closely by the two masses of metal, all veined with pipes and taps, and stepped under the great wooden framework which reached up to the open sky. Some way back, almost against the stone walls of the cavern, was a range of stalls. To these stalls they were led.

Each booth contained a seat, long fetters attached two to each opposite wall, and little else. Despite protests, they were chained hand and foot.

"This is just a filthy prison!" groaned Takeido. "I can't take much more of this."

"There are worse prisons than this all over Earth," said Burek.

"For that remark you will be reported," said Sygiek, with something of her old fire. "*Our* places of confinement are part of an elaborate judicial system, and are designed for re-education."

"More to the point," said Kordan, "observe that we have been promoted. We are no longer caged like animals but like human beings. They must keep us captive, inevitably, but they have installed us in a sacred place. What is more, I believe the president is apologizing."

"Apologizing!" said Takeido. He buried his face in his hands and began to laugh softly.

To judge by the leader's soothing tone, he was attempting something like an apology. He clapped his hands. An object was brought and handed to Kordan. He examined it.

"It is a foil-page book," he said. "It has some diagrams, so perhaps it is a textbook. Inevitably the language is some antique capitalist tongue. I've never seen the hieroglyphs before. It's not the Cyrillic or the Germanic, both of which I can decipher. It could be American."

As he handed it carelessly back, he said, "Thanks. Impossible to read."

"I doubt if he can read it either," said Dulcifer. "It's just a relic."

"That does not matter," said Burek. "He tries to show you that he reveres something which comes from off this world. You don't imagine they turn out foil-page books in this damned cave, do you?"

The book was taken away, the leader made another brief speech, bowed and withdrew, his retinue following.

X

They were left alone for the rest of the day, except when the aged crone brought them separate bowls of a watery soup, tasting of mint. The hours passed slowly and the benches were hard. Although they were able to look about over the doors of the cell and over the low walls which divided them one from another, the hours crawled by with awful sloth. They speculated about rescue, knowing that they would be missed at Unity and Peace City by now. Maintaining official optimism became particularly difficult during the long stretches of the afternoon.

The order in which they sat in their cells was: Burek, Kordan, Constanza, Takeido, Dulcifer, Sygiek.

"I will tell you all what I feel and think," Takeido burst out, when silence had ruled them for a long while. "I know that to do so is frowned upon, is either in bad taste or often punishable, but after all we shall never get back to the System, that's clear. First of all, I wish that I was lying by the river, with Rubyna Constanza in my arms, making love to her with her naked body against mine. Excuse me, Rubyna, but that's my devout wish."

Constanza said nothing. She bit her little finger and looked down.

" 'When one wolf howls, he howls for the whole pack,' " Burek quoted. He laughed.

After more silence, Takeido said, "So much for my desires. Now for my intellect. This may be even more distasteful to you. I have little scientific knowledge beyond my own discipline of exobotany, but I have speculated more than I have ever revealed. What I say, though based on new experience, is founded on old meditation.

"All right. Our lofty comrade, Academician Jerezy Kordan, is an official historian, but I daresay we have all acquired a little history, despite the many prohibitions. After all the élite knows how to bend its own rules, none better, eh? So. As I understand it, the old *homo sapiens* from which we sprang was haunted by many ghosts, all concerned with the inherited imperfections of their governance systems—I mean that becoming human entailed, in evolutionary terms, adding new control systems to old. So there was some built-in conflict, This, *homo sapiens* tried to explain in many ways throughout its history. A series of *meddlers* was invented, most of them external to man—projections, you might say, from inside to outside, for the greater comfort of the uncomfortable *sapiens*. Gods, ghosts, fates, devils, elves, fairies, spirits, golems. All were meddlers. Great religious and philosophical systems were built in order to account for physiological discomforts, many of them holding sway over men's minds for hundreds of years. The projections showed more durability than did brief *homo sapiens* individuals.

"As time went on, *sapiens* gained more control over nature but no more over himself. He could enslave the elements but remained himself a slave.

"During this period, the more advanced sections of *sapiens* changed their projections. New models were made to conform with a more sophisticated world-outlook. They embodied their discomforts in new metaphysical monsters—even in whole populated planets full of them. As we now know, such things cannot exist, but their imaginations were wild with discomfort. They also dreamed of perfect machines, things of metal which would not suffer from their internal disabilities. Robots, which we call radniks. Robots had only electronic circuits and no dreams, no internal confusions. Dreams, I should explain, were discharges of short-circuited nervous energy, generated by the uncomfortable conflict of the internal systems, which disturbed *sapiens'* sleep and were almost as important as sleep.

"Their entire science, though few of them realized it, was, in fact, incantatory, like the rituals we watched last night, designed to cast out the devils within. Eventually, they did design a perfect system. Of course, the prototype of a perfect political system had to come first, otherwise such experiments would have been forbidden by power-crazed governments.

"*Sapiens* did eventually see a way—through genetic engineering, and what we now term technoeugenics—to breed men and women without their own discomforts, their physiological handicaps. This is what we were saying yesterday.

"They bred us.

"That way, they also generated their own downfall. *Uniformis* had to take over their chaotic world.

"Well, comrades, you know what has happened since. Or what has *not* happened since. We have forged slowly on ever since we were invented. We have gone on and on, generation after generation. The old world has slowly died under our touch. We still keep a few animals, and, I believe, even a few *homo sapiens* in zoos. We are logical, and we understand the logic of controlling everything, from ourselves to the whole Solar System. Yet, apart from abolishing many *sapiens* features of life, like womb-birth and family and art and religion, what have we done? Nothing. Nothing. In a million years, we have in fact achieved less than *sapiens* achieved in a century or so."

"This is all rubbish," said Sygiek. "You are suffering from food-poisoning."

"You would naturally think it so, but you can spout later if you wish, Utopianist Millia Sygiek," said Takeido smoothly. "I have listened to your sort, you damned radniks, spouting all my life. Now I'm going to have my turn. I just want to say that there is another point of view to be put, and in the System it can never be put. There's no way of putting it. Know what I mean, comrades? If you speak out, you are an enemy of the system. Is our way of life then so insecure? Can one question make a whole statement collapse?

"Maybe so—when you look at the little we have accomplished. True, there's our method of gulf travel which *sapiens* could never have developed, since cratocalcs is a form of math beyond their mentalities—and beyond mine, I must add. Yet for all that, *sapiens* would by now have ventured farther than we. A million years of Biocom, and all we've done is entrench ourselves in the System like woodlice in an old log!"

In a coldly controlled voice, Kordan said, "Utopianist, your mind is dark indeed—and you shall have thorough treatment if we leave here alive—if that pitiable ritual we witnessed last night can provoke such subversive ferment!"

"No! No! Yes, yes, my mind is dark, you stinking intellectual pig, because the system forces us all to be separate from one another in the cursed name of Unity!" Takeido was kneeling up on his bench now as far as the shackles would allow him, and shouting across Constanza's cell at Kordan, who faced him whitely. Constanza cowered and covered her ears. "We can't trust each other because of the constant fear of betrayal—what the state calls conscience is just a vile pattern of betrayal. We can't trust each other —I dare to speak now merely because trust and betrayal are irrelevant in these circumstances. But you're right, yes, that ritual last night did make a ferment in my breast."

He was choking with emotion as he struck himself on his chest, rattling his chains. "I thought of the *endurance* of these people, of how they still care for their young, for instance, instead of rearing them like laboratory animals as we do. They survive in impossible conditions. I'll tell you— I'll tell you all, you numb utopians. I'll tell you, if a few hundred of *us* were set down on a deserted strip of Lysenka now, we should sit on our bottoms and talk and argue and bullshit until we perished. That would be our logic. We're just robots, radniks."

"Our talk is superior to their ritual," commented Burek. "Sit down, Takeido, sit down and shut up. Yours is an immature argument. You do no good to anyone."

Takeido broke out anew.

"Ha, you wouldn't support me, would you, Utopianist Burek? You are just an isolated individual posing as an individualist to retain some shred of self-respect. Yet you can neither give nor receive help—just the sort of puppet the system wants!" He twisted round the other way and shouted to Dulcifer. "And what about *you*, Vul Dulcifer? Do you support me? Every now and again you say little daring things! In our hearts we know why—yes, we know why! You're an agent provocateur, a member of the stinking rotten USRP! Don't bother to deny it. I'm not afraid to say what everyone has guessed."

"They've guessed wrong if so," said Dulcifer. "Sit down, comrade—we've got enough troubles without your adding to them."

"Yes, please sit down, Ian," said Constanza.

"I'll sit down," said Takeido. "I'll sit down because Rubyna asks me, and she's the only decent person here. I'll sit down, but first I'll tell you my great idea. It's a way we might break the impossible stranglehold that Biocom has on everyone in the System. I'll say it whether you support me or not.

"We should forget our carefully taught prejudices and see that these savages here are to be admired. Yes, admired! They should not be obliterated. We should see that they are preserved. More than that, they should be taken back, every last man, woman and child, and established in a large settlement on Earth or Mars. Not all the degenerate animal-forms; simply those tribes—this one and any others like it—who have managed to retain their humanity over more than a million years in the face of impossible odds. I believe we need them. After a million stultifying years of World Unity, I believe we need *sapiens* as they once thought they needed us. That's all."

"That's quite enough," said Constanza, sharply. "You speak heresy. Sit down."

The tone of her voice deflated Takeido. He slumped back on his bench and said no more.

"There's much one could say," said Kordan. His voice died; he did not say it.

Nobody else spoke for a long while. Most of them drifted off to sleep. Only Sygiek sat upright, scarcely moving, looking ahead into the gloom of the cavern.

She it was who saw the beginning of the end of the day. The clouds parted overhead, the sky faded to pearl, and the cave-dwellers began to return to their warrens. More dead animals were brought in. Children began to run about. Priests moved again in the temple, candles were lit. Men marched in with torches, there were the sounds of voices, shouts. The fires were stoked and an aroma of cooking filled the air.

She turned and roused Dulcifer. One by one, the others stirred and sat up, groaning with discomfort.

Dulcifer looked over the cell wall at Takeido.

"Utopianist Takeido, despite your insults and exaggerations, I was interested in what you had to say about inadequacies of the system and our needing *homo sapiens.*"

"Forget it. I know what your interest is worth." Takeido would not look up.

"Your youthfulness makes you believe that because the system's only slowly forging ahead something is wrong. When you grow a good deal older, your beliefs will perform the same mirror-reversal that mine did; you will come to understand that it was *sapiens'* mad unchecked development which was the symptom of something wrong. I daresay that, as you claim, *sapiens* would have overrun half the galaxy by now. But remember what a mess they made of Earth! Don't get sentimental about them. Think what a mess they would have made of the galaxy. No, our cautious way is better.

"But I cannot hope to persuade you to my view any more than you can persuade me to yours; it is not argument which changes our minds on such matters, but time."

Takeido shook his head and looked at his manacled hands. In a low voice he said, "I suppose you are equally incapable of accepting the argument that we are in danger of becoming exactly the sort of robots that *sapiens* envisioned?"

When some seconds had passed, and Dulcifer did not reply, Kordan said, "Whether or not we leave this cave alive, there is no reason why we should tolerate seditious discussion. The robots are living here, going through their mumbo-jumbo every day and night.

"You find a hunting life exciting, no doubt, Takeido, because you are young. But there is more challenge in the way of life our system has set itself. Our challenge is existential. It cannot be cured temporarily by a full belly or a wench. We suppress our self, we surrender our identity, for the greater benefit of society and the state. We are aware of the cost of doing so, we are also aware that the condition of life is tragic. But that is the way we have

98

chosen and we must pursue it throughout life—without pity for our own weaknesses, or for the weaknesses of others."

"Such as mine," said Takeido.

"Such as yours," agreed Kordan. "If we do return to the System, we shall meet again when you are on trial. I shall be in the witness box."

Sneering, Takeido raised a finger at him.

Again silence fell, and they watched as more figures entered the cavern. The patch of clouded sky overhead was growing dark. Cave-dwellers were entering the foreparts of the temple, parading solemnly round with candles, saluting the priests.

"The monotony of life!" exclaimed Sygiek. "We seem to have been imprisoned here for years. The region outside must be surveyed by satellites if the strike is over, and by flycraft from Peace City . . . If only one of us could get out . . ."

"Let's see what happens during this evening's ceremonies," said Dulcifer. "I have a feeling that they are going to make use of us. We may be able to snatch a chance then. Never despair, Millia, never despair."

As on the previous evening, family groups were entering; there were women among them with babies at the breast, and small children who kept silent. The complicated charades followed, meaningless to the observers. Then the people joined together into a unified group, ascended the steps, and entered the temple.

They bowed low and began to rub the palms of their hands on the two solid masses of machinery which stood below the central wooden scaffolding.

"Could those metal things be the engines of the colonist ship?" asked Constanza.

"After all this while, the original engines would have rusted away," said Burek. "These could be replicas. I had the thought that this is a kind of dumb-show about repairing the machines. Do you think so, Dulcifer? You're an engineer as well as a part-time philosopher."

"I'm an engineer but I don't know what goes on in those savages' scruffy heads. I can see what goes on in their bodies. They are a poor undernourished lot."

They had plenty of time to observe thin shanks, protruding bones, and sore-infected legs before the ceremony played itself out and the company retired. Now the family groups assembled round the central fires. Again the white-haired woman in flowing robes came forth and proceeded to relate a long story. "Can it be the same story?" asked Sygiek. "Surely they can't bear it every night. It must be different."

"Indoctrination," said Takeido, succinctly. It was the first word he had spoken for some while.

Eventually the food came on. It was served as before by the women in aprons. The man with the bag across his stomach came and collected tokens from everyone.

"Yes, you see—capitalism!" exclaimed Constanza. "They have to—to make a money payment for everything. That is their god!"

Food was brought to the prisoners. They were exempt from payment. This evening, there was a bowl for each. They ate without comment, avoiding each other's gaze. Even Constanza ate.

The evening wore on. After the food came another circus act, featuring two creatures with long necks, who cried as they ran about before being killed. When it was time for the next part of the ceremony, the leader appeared with his retinue. Everyone stood. A gong sounded. The leader raised an imperious hand in greeting.

He walked grandly through the temple and halted before the stalls housing the six prisoners. Striking a posture, he addressed them loudly, so that everyone present could hear. Then he motioned to his men to release them, and their shackles were struck from them.

Takeido immediately flung his arms about Rubyna Constanza.

"Dearest Rubyna, how I have longed to hold you! Tell me you understand what I was saying when I made those mad speeches."

"I am not a fool. I understand, Ian Takeido. You hate everything we believe best."

"You do not condemn me?" He drew back from her.

"When we express our own opinions, we must inevitably suffer for them. That is not *my* law—it is *the* law." That was all she said. She stood away from him and smoothed her crumpled red uniform.

"Don't use that awful word 'inevitably.' That's Kordan's word." That was all he said. He moved toward her.

The guards separated them.

Sygiek said to Kordan, quietly, "We must trust each other, Jerezy Kordan. I approve your straight speaking to Takeido. If you plan some positive action, of course I shall support it."

"That is a change of attitude for you, Millia Sygiek." He looked at her sternly and pursed his lips. "You have given me little support—in the matter of handing over the gun, for instance."

"Then pride yourself on having taken care of that item." She touched his arm. "You and I are proud people, and not entirely incompatible, as the computer properly decided. Our incompatibilities can be a matter for later discussion."

He looked her hard in the eyes. "We shall see whether what you say turns out to be a promise or a threat. Meanwhile, you must consider it your duty to support my leadership."

She sighed. "As you correctly state, we suppress our identities for the common good. We must do so now."

The guards separated them as well.

Dulcifer said to Burek, "If I have the chance to make a sudden move, I rely on you to back me up, Che Burek."

"Everyone finds me very reliable," said Burek. "That is how I have survived for so long. You saw how I swallowed my anger beneath Takeido's insults. 'An elephant takes no notice of a gnat.' "

"I'm asking you to be a *man*, not a confounded elephant."

The guards also separated them.

They were all led forward in a body.

XI

The priests had been preparing a platform. It stood in clear view of everyone, under the tall wooden scaffolding. With courteous gestures, some of the priests encouraged the captives to mount it. They did so. A low murmur of anticipation rose from the assembled cave-dwellers.

Constanza stood next to Kordan and clutched his arm. Her face was pale. "We are to be either honored or executed," she said.

"Don't be alarmed, Rubyna Constanza. These savages have recognized our qualities and hope for something from us. Stand by me."

Looking up, the six saw that the opening in the cavern roof was directly above them. The adjustable chair-couch stood nearby. The scaffolding was perhaps a crude imitation of some bygone device from which the capitalists had used to launch their rockets; so decided Sygiek. No stars could be seen through the roof opening tonight—but there were strange flashes of light which she could not understand. Probably a storm was brewing.

The leader of the cave-dwellers began another oration, lifting his arms. His voice roared out, echoing through the space. The mass of people, urging their children before them, surged forward, until they stood on the steps of the temple. Their faces were eager.

The platform began to move unsteadily. It lifted a centimeter or two from the ground. Fire-crackers began to burst underneath.

"They understand that we are from another world," said Kordan. "They are using us as a teaching example. Stand steady. We shall come to no harm. Stand firm!"

"I'm not planning to be an example to any bunch of savages!" said Dulcifer.

The platform lifted slowly, crackers still exploding underneath. It was hauled up by ropes attached to each corner. To one side, concealed from the audience, eight priests tugged lustily at a winch.

When the platform was a meter or more in the air, it came to a halt. The people cried out. Dulcifer leaped upward and outward. He seized hold of the wooden scaffolding, swinging himself up. The leader of the cave-dwellers, who had been conducting the ascent as if it were music, gave a shout of anger. He jumped forward, pulling out a sword, brandishing it.

He ran to the scaffolding, eyes and voice raised toward Dulcifer. The priests in consternation let go of the winch handles. The platform crashed back to the ground, sending its five passengers sprawling. Dulcifer drew a gun from his pocket and fired downward.

Kordan pulled himself to his feet, face livid. "Come back, Dulcifer! You stole the gun from me when I was asleep last night, you deviant! I thought Sygiek had retrieved it. Don't shoot!"

"You're useless without the system, Kordan, get back!"

Dulcifer fired another shot and then began rapidly to climb.

"Keep going, comrade!" Takeido shouted.

The tribal leader staggered and fell back into Kordan's arms. Sygiek ran forward to help Kordan. Between them they held the leader up. He staggered and thrashed his arms about. His face was distorted with pain. Blood gushed from between his lips and, with a great cry, he died.

The whole company rose and began to advance up the temple steps toward the utopians.

Dulcifer took one last look at the milling scene below. He had reached the top of the scaffolding. It swayed dangerously back and forth. As he balanced on the upper spars, legs wide, his head rose within a shallow chimney of rock leading to the world above. The chimney was little more than one and a half meters wide and two in depth. Beyond it, dark cloud scudded in a dark sky.

He tensed himself. He sprang. All the ferocious energy of his body was thrown into clinging to the rock. Stones and rubble fell away beneath his hands, but he managed with outstretched arms to wedge himself into the chimney. One foot found a hold in the side. Breath burst from his lungs, sweat seamed his face, he heaved himself up the chimney.

After a timeless interval, his head appeared in open air. His shoulders came through. With a gasp of relief, he got his arms through and hauled himself out on sloping ground. He lay where he was for a minute, clutching his bleeding palms in his armpits. Then he rose, staggering slightly, and looked round.

He was free.

The hole from which he had emerged was protected by boulders. In the darkness, he could distinguish little of his surroundings. But the breeze that visited his cheek, the fresh flavor of the air, a distant sound of running water, the cool impression on his temples, even the feel of gravelly ground under his feet—all these things brought him an immediate rejoicing sense of the planet, as a man may, on an instant, recall a lost love. He raised his arms and clenched his fists to the skies and could scarcely check himself from sending up a great cheer. Grunting, he sucked the night air into his lungs.

He brought his fists down and started to pick his way downhill.

Once he was free of the encircling boulders, lights met his eye. He halted, confused. Two searchlights were weaving and interlocking ahead.

"Hey, who's there?" he called. "Friend or foe?"

Seconds later, a cratobatic matboat was speeding through the air toward him. It stopped, hovering just above the ground, and two WUA officers with the World Unity symbol on their caps jumped down and slapped him on the back. Quickly they exchanged names and explanations. They helped Dulcifer climb aboard and settle into the exposed bucket seats. Two WUA soldiers and a man in the grim black uniform of the USRP were already aboard.

"We thought you'd never get to us," Dulcifer said. "Is the strike still on?"

The USRP official spoke. "There was no strike, Utopianist Dulcifer—get that clear. Merely a little technical problem, now disposed of. For the rest, we have come fast and efficiently. You should not question that."

Dulcifer laughed. *"You* should try being captured by cannibals some time!"

"We had a large area to search," one of the WUA officers said. "Since you were taken underground, our instruments could get no fix on you." He passed a flask to Dulcifer, and clapped his shoulder. "We are glad to be in time, Vul Dulcifer."

"You may not be in time, as far as the rest are concerned. Move down to the river and I'll try to show you the way in through the cliffs. Can we blow right in on this matboat?"

"You bet. No trouble."

"Good. Let's go. Every second counts." He took a deep and satisfying swig of the fiery liquid in the flask.

One of the soldiers was already transmitting information to two other scouting matboats nearby. They all converged on lower ground. On the far side of the river, a tracked land-vehicle waited. Following the course of the river, the matboat sped through the air, playing its searchlight on the cliff-face. The other matboats followed.

The cliff-face was peppered with holes, each looking alike. There was no sign of life. The area appeared uninhabited.

"They pull up the ladders at night," said Dulcifer, and began to sweat. In anxiety, he pounded on his knees.

He caught sight of a bridge, present as a slab across the dull glitter of water below.

"That could be our bridge. Turn in here. Try a tunnel about ten meters up the cliff-face."

The flat craft made a smart left turn and headed straight toward the cliff. The pilot punched buttons. The mountain swallowed them. Hardly slowing, the matboat forged straight into a tunnel and then paused. Dulcifer sank back in alarm and covered his head.

A wash of light, roughly circular, preceded them as

they moved forward again. The way looked promising. There were tribal sentinels here, who ran in panic before them or passed themselves to the walls, crying in terror, hiding their eyes.

"More animals!" laughed one of the officers. "We are on the right track." He brought up a weapon and began to fire. A sentinel fell struggling and was lost behind in the darkness. The soldiers cheered.

Dulcifer grabbed the officer's arm. "Don't shoot them down. They aren't animals."

The tunnel curved, branched, twisted left. A barricade rushed toward them. A blaze of orange light from the front of their craft and the timbers disappeared in smoke. They swept through a cloud of angry ash and burst into the main cavern, lights blazing.

Crowds of cave-dwellers, snatching up their children, ran in all directions. Screams rang out. The officers raised their guns again.

"Don't shoot!" cried Dulcifer.

The matboat stopped a few centimeters above the ground. Officers, soldiers, Dulcifer, jumped out.

In the temple stood Sygiek, Kordan, Constanza, Burek and Takeido, momentarily paralyzed in a tableau. The dead tribal leader lay at their feet. The leader's retinue and various priests crouched nearby in attitude of worship. The rest of the congregation, now breaking away to run for their lives, had also been in kneeling positions.

"You are all right? We are in time?" called Dulcifer, concernedly, hurrying forward to his friends. "My dear Millia Sygiek—you are safe!"

Sygiek had drawn herself up against Kordan, who clasped her arm. She stood tensely, regarding Dulcifer with her grey eyes as he approached. Her face was expressionless. Dignitaries and priests gave way before him, but she did not stir.

"You're a mad dog, Utopianist Dulcifer," said Kordan, putting out a hand. "You have broken the law with your use of firearms—that and all your other offenses will not go disregarded, be sure of that."

Dulcifer ignored him and looked intensely at Sygiek.

"Millia, speak to me! Our ordeal is over."

"They fell down before us. They worshiped us. They

accepted us as gods," she said, in an amazed way. "How little they comprehend. And how little we comprehend about ourselves."

"Leave her alone, Dulcifer," said Kordan. "When you shot their leader, what was to stop them tearing us apart in revenge? A lot you cared! By good fortune, we were so firmly embedded in a godlike rôle in their ritual that they accepted the killing as justified, as a sacrifice, and did us no harm. We could all have been dead by now."

Dulcifer tapped him derisively on the chest. "You've done little enough to save your skin, Kordan. Think yourself lucky that there's someone in this universe fool enough to mistake you for a god." He turned to Sygiek and embraced her, holding her against his clumsy body, stroking her hair.

"They spared us," she exclaimed, in the same dazed voice as before. "They must worship power and see us as all-powerful. Why else should they spare us?"

"That's a law of the universe—worshiping power," said Dulcifer. "But I did worry for you, Millia Sygiek, just in case the laws of the universe happened to fail for once. Fortunately, there is also such a thing as mercy."

"Mercy . . ." Sygiek came out of her daze and clutched him fiercely. "Yes, even I have heard of mercy, Vul. I want to talk to you. Properly talk. When we get back home. Let's dare to speak to each other."

He clasped her, out of words, as her eyes shone into his.

As the dwellers of the caves stole away, two more mat-boats arrived in the cavern. Soldiers jumped out with guns at the ready, partly encircling the six tourists. The tourists were embracing and congratulating each other on surviving. Burek's rumbling laugh sounded. Officers and soldiers were cheering.

But Rubyna Constanza broke from Ian Takeido's grasp with an angry exclamation and walked down the temple steps toward the official of the USRP. Takeido made to follow her, then stopped. Her name burst from his lips. "Rubyna Constanza!" Pale of face, she did not look back.

The other tourists turned, caught by a sudden chill in the air. The soldiers fell silent.

The USRP official, his boots twinkling in high polish,

moved forward to meet Constanza. His seamed face was creased into a smile, his hands were outstretched.

"Greetings! There will be much official relief to know that you are still alive and safe, Official Rubyna Constanza," he said. "We have searched ceaselessly for you ever since rescuing the others of your wrecked bus party yesterday."

Constanza touched his hands. She straightened her back and spoke in a voice the others hardly recognized.

"You took far too long. We have been much humiliated, Official Gunnar Gastovich, humiliated. Somebody must be held responsible."

"My apologies, Comrade Official. Deepest apologies. The strike obstructed our purposes—the guilty parties will be dealt with. Of that you can be sure. We will transport you back to Peace City at once."

Ignoring his remark, Constanza straightened her uniform and turned to confront the tourists.

"Official Gunnar Gastovich, I order you to arrest these five tourists, Ian Takeido, Che Burek, Vul Dulcifer, Jerezy Kordan, and the woman Millia Sygiek. Take them into custody at once. I shall make a full report when I return to Peace City. I have uncovered a conspiracy against our beloved system."

Gastovich snapped his fingers and the soldiers began to move in.

"She's insane!" called Kordan. "Nobody is more loyal to the system than I. I am an Academician, an honored and respected Academician of the IPUS. You cannot arrest me. You shall be punished for this, Comrade Rubyna Constanza, when I get back to Earth. I demand to know the charges."

Takeido was weeping and calling her name.

"Be quiet, Ian Takeido," Constanza said severely. "You are showing manifestations of guilt, which are duly noted. The others will have to testify to your lengthy polemics against the state, which carry a maximum penalty. As for the rest of you—" She raised her finger and pointed it three times at Sygiek, Kordan and Dulcifer. "These three persons came to this planet for subversive purposes. They are members of a cell and shared possession of an illegal weapon, as will be testified."

Burek shook his fist. "Don't leave me out of your roll

of honor, you witch! I stand by my comrades. I hate the USRP as much as they do, and I will be punished as they are."

"Silence!" bawled Gastovich.

"The charges against these criminals," said Constanza. Her voice faltered and she started the sentence again. "The charges against these criminals include conspiracy, sedition, hostile logic, deformed thought-processes, misapplication of history, free discussion of Classified matters, treachery against the party, pessimism, collusion with traitors, and intent to conspire with degenerate capitalists who scheme to take over control of this planet. All five are enemies of the system—guard them closely!"

She swayed as she spoke. Gastovich steadied her. He gestured angrily at the WUA officers, who were hesitating. Even the soldiers had paused, confronting the five accused where they stood in a tight group on the lowest step of the temple.

"What are you waiting for? Arrest those scum!"

The gun was in Dulcifer's hands. He pushed Sygiek behind him. He held the gun at arm's length, aiming it at the black-clad Reason Police official.

"Stay where you are, everyone, or that piece of shit dies. Officers of the WUA, you are honorable men, I ask you—"

One shot rang out. An officer from the third matboat had fired from the hip. Dulcifer back into the arms of Millia Sygiek, dropping his gun, clasping his shoulder. The soldiers rushed forward.

Ignoring the shouts and cries, Gastovich bowed to Constanza. He gestured toward his craft. "The prisoners shall travel in one of the other boats. You will please accompany me. You have done good work and honors will be bestowed upon you. Now—the sooner we get back to civilization the better."

The five prisoners were goaded or carried into the other machines. Engines started. The craft turned in perfect formation. They sped from the cavern, through the tunnels, and into the night of Lysenka II.

THE BEST IN SCIENCE FICTION
AND FANTASY FROM
AVON ◆ BOOKS

URSULA K. LE GUIN

The Lathe of Heaven	43547	1.95
The Dispossessed	51284	2.50

ISAAC ASIMOV

Foundation	50963	2.25
Foundation and Empire	52357	2.25
Second Foundation	52290	2.25
The Foundation Trilogy (Large Format)	50856	6.95

ROGER ZELAZNY

Doorways in the Sand	49510	1.75
Creatures of Light and Darkness	35956	1.50
Lord of Light	44834	2.25
The Doors of His Face The Lamps of His Mouth	38182	1.50
The Guns of Avalon	31112	1.50
Nine Princes in Amber	51755	1.95
Sign of the Unicorn	53132	1.95
The Hand of Oberon	51318	1.75
The Courts of Chaos	47175	1.7

Include 50¢ per copy for postage and handling,
allow 4-6 weeks for delivery.

Avon Books, Mail Order Dept.
224 W. 57th St., N.Y., N.Y. 10019

SF 2-8